MW01174836

CROSSING
THE
LINE

Feb 16/93.

For Paul,

Hope you have some
poetry I can come across
sometime.

CROSSING
THE
LINE

Short Stories
by

DAVID H. ELIAS

Orca Book Publishers

Canadian Cataloguing in Publication Data
Elias, David H., 1949–
    Crossing the line

    ISBN 0-920501-86-9
    I. Title.
PS8559.L53C7 1992   C813'.54   C92-0916155
PR9199.3E45C7 1992

Publication assistance provided by The Canada Council.

Cover design and illustration by Terry Gallagher, Doowah Design.

Orca Book Publishers
PO Box 5626, Station B
Victoria, BC Canada
V8R 6S4

Printed and bound in Canada.

For Len,
somewhere on the other side

———————

The author wishes to acknowledge the assistance of The
Canada Council.

Earlier versions of these stories first appeared in *Secrets
From the Orange Couch, Manitoba Myriad: An Anthology of
Poetry and Prose*, and *Western People*.

Table of Contents

Take it moment by moment, and you will find
that we are all, as I've said before,
bugs in amber.

Kurt Vonnegut, Jr.
from *Slaughterhouse Five*

The Laughter of the Devil

———

The hyena paces back and forth in an intoxicating, suffocating rhythm of precise repetition. The large head swivels between bulky shoulders, while the shrunken, shaggy hindquarters follow like an afterthought.

At the far end of the platform, the front legs stiffen, the massive muzzle searching the air in a sniffing posture. It stays there for only a split second before the snout brushes against *the weathered boards of the shelter, the hind legs buckle, and the animal throws itself around to trot in the opposite direction.*

There is a patch of new wood where the nose rubbed, and another one just like it on the far side. There are more patches along the floor of the platform, where the huge paws fall in the same place each time.

When people walk by tomorrow, or next month, or next year, the ritual will be exactly the same. Brilliant.

"You go ahead," shouted Steven. "I'll catch up."

"But it'll be time to go soon," yelled Bill, walking backwards.

Steven waved him on, then called after him, "Save me a seat on the bus."

Bill turned and ran to catch the others.

Steven watched him run out of sight around the artificial rocks of the polar bear cages. It wasn't any big deal, not spending every minute with him. It was just that today they had been allowed to tag along with the older boys. They had been just one big gang, strolling from cage to cage, taking it all in—until he had spotted Trudy.

He watched her now, sitting on the bench, with the other girls standing over her. She was waving at them, shooing them away. They were protesting, telling her they'd wait. But Steven knew they had waited too many times already, and there wasn't much time left.

They saw Steven coming toward them. One of them pointed and said something, and then they turned and ran off together in a cluster of noise.

It wasn't that he worried about her. She liked to be

alone. She often said so. She had a way of being alone that was different from anybody he knew. It wasn't angry or hurt or sad. It was a calm and gentle kind of solitude.

But this was the city. Being alone in the country felt kind of natural, but in the city, it just felt strange. And besides, this was her first time.

"I don't mind sitting by myself," she said when he sat down next to her. "I really don't."

"I know."

They sat together in silence. There didn't seem to be anyone around. Everyone was someplace else. What if they had all gone home? What if they hadn't heard the bell? What if the others were on the bus right now, laughing and singing on their way back to Haskenfeld?

He glanced quickly at Trudy to see if she had detected his alarm. There wasn't much he could hide from her. Maybe that was why he didn't spend more time with her.

But then he spotted Miss Nickel over by the washrooms. She was holding a little boy up to the water fountain. She put him down and pointed to the door. The boy disappeared inside, and she picked up another child. Steven let his shoulders fall and took a deep breath.

"Miss Nickel is over there," he said.

"I know, but I'm staying here. I'm not a baby, you know."

"I think I've seen everything," he said.

"Me too."

"The monkeys were the best."

"I guess."

"Did you see the hyena?" asked Steven.

Trudy's round face became oval. She turned quickly. "They have a hyena here?"

"Right through there. Didn't you see it?"

"Is it far?"

"No, just a few minutes."

"Can we go see it? Please?"

"I thought you were tired."

"I was, but I'm okay now. Besides, we can just take it slow. I'm okay as long as we take it slow."

"Come on."

They started out along the path. Everything seemed so quiet. A crow rattled out of the trees and ragged at them from above. Trudy's shoes clumped hollow against the stones. Steven turned his eyes down at them.

They were more like boots, really, especially the left one, with that extra-thick sole. It looked so big and clumsy stuck on the end of that tiny pale leg. He remembered picking it up for the first time. It weighed even more than he had expected.

He thought about the grey moccasins his mother bought for him in winter. They were much cheaper than shoes, and they weighed practically nothing. You could slide along the snow almost like skating. And with two or three pairs of socks, your feet stayed cosy warm.

He wondered how warm Trudy's shoes were in the winter, and how it felt to walk through the snow in them.

When they got to the hyena's cage the first thing Trudy did was read the sign. "It says right here," she pointed, "sometimes called the Laughing Hyena, the sound of its cry has been compared to *high-stir* . . .

his-stare-rickle laughter." She turned to Steven. "Just like Mama said." They stood side by side, watching the hyena pace back and forth across the wooden platform.

Their mother had a collection of stories that she told and retold. Steven had heard them all many times, but with each telling the images in his mind grew stronger. He knew which story Trudy was thinking of—the one about the missionary family in Africa.

This family had a little baby that the mother always carried around. She didn't want to leave it anywhere because there were lots of bugs and small animals and they didn't have a regular house but more like a hut to sleep in.

One night she put the baby down in the hut for a few minutes to go and get something from outside. When she came back, the baby was gone. She knew right away what had happened to it.

She called her missionary husband and they started to look for the baby. It was dark and they had to use torches. They could hear the baby crying. But when they got to where the sound was coming from, there wouldn't be anything there.

After a while they couldn't hear the baby anymore, but they could hear someone laughing. But it wasn't really someone laughing. It was a hyena. A laughing hyena had stolen the baby.

The father got his gun and they ran after the hyena. But they could never seem to get near it. Then the father went crazy and started laughing too, just like the hyena.

But the mother kept right on looking. She searched all night long, but she never found the baby.

Steven had often imagined what that laughter must have sounded like—the hyena and the missionary—together in the dark. It must have sounded like the laughter of the devil.

———

"I found something else," said Trudy. Steven felt her tapping his arm.

He turned back quickly. "What? Oh." They had been playing a game. Trudy was always making up games to play. In this game, they had to take turns finding things the hyena did each time he made a trip back and forth across the platform. Steven had turned away when he heard the other boys. Now they were over by the monkeys, laughing and pointing up into the cages.

"I thought you liked this game," said Trudy.

"I do." Steven tried to sound convincing. "Show me what you found. I want to see it."

"Okay, this is really good. I don't know how we missed it. Now waatch . . . waaaatch . . . there! Did you see it?"

Steven waited for her to tell him. His heart just wasn't in it anymore.

"It's his paw. Watch again. Here he comes . . . and . . . . . . there! See what he does? He hangs his front paw over the edge of the platform in the same place every time. Now it's your turn," she said triumphantly.

She looked up at him. She could see in his eyes that the interest was gone. It wasn't any use.

"I don't feel like playing anymore. I think we'd better

find the others."

"Can't we just stay a few more minutes? Please."

"Okay, just a little longer. I don't see what the big attraction is."

He looked around the enclosure. All that separated them from the hyena was a low fence of two thin wires that ran along a shallow concrete trench, perhaps three feet wide. An average-sized dog could easily have cleared it in one leap.

"You know what I wonder?" said Steven. "I wonder how come he stays in there at all. This sure isn't much of a cage. All he has to do is jump."

"Maybe he doesn't want to get out," Trudy responded. "Maybe he's like the cows and chickens on the farm. They don't run away as long as you feed them."

"He's nothing like that. He's wild. He must hate it in there."

"Then why doesn't he jump?"

"Maybe he has. Maybe he tried and didn't make it."

"Well, at least he tried."

"He probably can't jump very far with his back end all shrivelled up like that."

Trudy looked down at her leg. "Shrivelled," she said quietly. Steven wished he hadn't used the word. Trudy lifted her head and smiled up at him.

That smile. Where did it come from?

"I wonder why God made him that way?" she said.

"The same reason he made you that way, I guess." There was no point pretending now. "Trudy, have you ever asked God to fix your leg?"

Her smile disappeared. "Why do you ask things like that?"

"I didn't mean anything. I just wondered."

"You're always wondering about something." They were quiet. The hyena paced off the silent seconds. Without turning to face him, she said, "No."

"No?" echoed Steven. "You mean no you never asked him?"

"And I never will."

"Oh."

"I'm like this for a reason."

Steven played with the paint chips on the steel railing.

"God has a plan," she continued. "That's what Grampa says."

"But maybe God's plan is for you to ask him. Maybe his plan is for you to ask him and then he'll make you better, but he can't do it until you ask him." The ideas tumbled out. There was no stopping them. He didn't mind it so much during the day, but it was worse at night. "And if you did ask him, and he didn't do it, then maybe his plan was just for you to ask him, but not for you to get better. But how do you know unless you ask him?"

"I want to go now," said Trudy. "I want to go home."

He should never have started. It was just that things had never worked out between God and him.

Long ago, the Sunday school teacher had told everyone in class how they could take Jesus into their hearts and be saved. How their lives would be changed if only they would let it happen.

He had listened with such hope—had wanted it more than anything else in the world. He had wanted it because of the nights when he awoke in the darkness to his father's voice, muffled and angry behind the closed door. He'd wanted it for his mother, wailing quietly through the wall.

He'd wanted it for the waiting. There was always the waiting. Waiting to hear his mother's quiet sobs through the walls. It always ended that way.

Sometimes she cried right away, which was good. Other times it seemed like hours before his father could make her cry. Then he would wince under the smack of a hand on his mother's face, or maybe just her arm. It was probably just her arm. Or maybe it was one of those fake slaps that you could trick somebody with where you just smacked your own hand—but he didn't think so.

Anyway, it made her cry, which meant it was over, and he could try to sleep again.

The Sunday school teacher had said you had to believe, really believe, that Jesus would come into your heart, and that was called faith. You had to have a lot of that.

He'd asked the teacher, "How do you get it?"

The Sunday school teacher's clean young face had come full against his, her hands in her lap. "Pray," she said, "pray as often as you can."

All through that summer Steven had prayed. He prayed before he went to bed. He prayed when he got up in the morning. He prayed during the day when he thought no one was watching.

Sometimes he prayed in the coal shed, because one Sunday they had read in the Bible that you should go into a closet to pray, so a coal shed had to be pretty close. In fact, a coal shed might even be better, because when you got down on your knees, the sharp pieces dug into your skin. There was always a lot of pain and suffering in the Bible, so that had to be good for something.

He always prayed the same way. "Jesus, come into my heart. I want you for my personal saviour. Come into my heart and forgive all my sins. Please, Jesus, please."

At night he would lie awake for hours praying, waiting to be saved, waiting for Jesus to come down into his heart. When he finally fell asleep he would dream about being saved. In his dream he was standing in a crowd of people, listening to Jesus. He could never actually hear the words Jesus was saying, but it didn't matter. Everyone looked like the people in the Bible story books—faces shiny and clean and impossibly happy.

All summer he'd prayed, and waited. He'd wanted it more than anything—except maybe for Trudy's leg to get better and for her not to feel so tired all the time—but it never happened.

A couple of times he thought it might be happening, but it would always turn out to be something else: the sun on his face, or an oriole singing, or a cool breeze out of the hills. And he would realize that it wasn't Jesus after all. It was just being alive that day.

———

Steven stared blankly into the long grass that grew undisturbed along the far side of the trench. The hyena had not stopped pacing for one second.

He shouldn't have asked Trudy so many questions. It wasn't fair.

"Anyway, it doesn't matter about the hyena," he said. "Even if he did make it, where would he go?"

They heard the bell, and turned to go. It was time to leave for the long bus ride home. Miss Nickel was ringing the bell high above her head. Then she gave it to one of the little children, who took it in both hands and shook it wildly back and forth.

The children gathered round, some not even reaching her waist, others taller than she was. Steven and Trudy walked toward them. Behind them, the hyena, one paw over the edge of the platform, made its turn.

Trudy placed her tiny hand in Steven's. "We're not like the others, are we?" she said.

If their backs had not been turned, they would have seen that the hyena froze for a moment, staring out at them, before continuing on its way.

Steven thought of the song they had often sung in Sunday school:

> *Jesus loves me this I know.*
> *For the Bible tells me so.*
> *Little ones to him belong.*
> *They are weak but he is strong.*

For some reason he felt like singing it. But just to himself, in his mind, as he let her hold his hand, he changed the words and sang silently:

> *Trudy loves me, this I know.*

Hidden Places

A glint of light up in the hills caught Steven's eye. A car was throwing up dust, dipping in and out of view, as it wound its way down into the valley. They would have met eventually, where the road flattened out against the prairie floor, if Steven hadn't turned north and headed for Klassen's General Store.

Bill would be out riding with him, if he hadn't had

so many chores to do. Steven had even offered to help, but Bill had only looked down at the new bike and said, "I can't go today. Pa wants me here. Maybe tomorrow."

When Steven got to the store, he leaned the bike carefully against the front wall before he went inside. Mr. Klassen was busy behind the front counter, slicing up a slab of halva with the same knife he always used. It had been sharpened too many times and there was an awkward curve in the blade.

"If you came for the mail, you're too early," the storekeeper said without looking up.

Steven sat down on a wooden crate and listened to the hum of the drink cooler. It was never too warm in the store, no matter how hot it was outside.

"That's okay." Steven waved him off. "I can wait. I'm not in any hurry." The scent of jellied cookies and oranges settled around him.

Mr. Klassen glanced up for a second. "Hasn't your Papa got any *oaabahyt* for you on that big farm of his?"

"Not today," Steven answered foolishly.

There was never any work for him. He woke every morning to the sound of augers pushing grain, tractors hauling machinery, shovels banging against each other—to a day he was not part of. There were plenty of hired hands to do the work. Some of them were boys not much older than he was. If he was at the table when they came in to eat, he would finish quickly and leave. Somehow he just didn't feel right eating with them. It would be different if his father had given him a job to do. He would do a good day's work with the other hands and then he would eat with them—the way they ate—with the same righteous appetite. His father ate after everyone else had finished. Steven watched him sometimes, chewing his food tediously, without enthusiasm. He had never seen his father really enjoy a plate of food.

Tires churned across the gravel and Mr. Klassen looked up to see who was out front. There was a final scuff as the wheels locked to a stop. A door slammed, then another, not as loudly. The little bell tinkled over the door.

A lean man in a wide-brimmed leather hat stepped out of the daylight. He was unshaven, and there were shadows around his sunken eyes. His shirt and pants were the colour of grease. When he stepped over to the counter, Mr. Klassen stopped cutting and laid the knife on the counter.

The man was followed by a boy about Steven's age. He was dressed like his father, but with a bare head, shaved close, and dirty bare feet. The man pointed to the sacks of sugar and flour stacked up near the back of the store. The boy walked by Steven and picked up a fifty-pound sack of Robin Hood flour. He threw it across his shoulder, walked back, and laid it across the counter. When he returned for a sack of sugar, Steven noticed bright patches of ringworm on his arms.

The man walked up to the counter and spoke in a quiet, low voice. Mr. Klassen got out three tins of Players tobacco and three packs of Vogue papers and put them in a bag. The boy stood beside his father, looking down at the box of halva.

The man reached into his pocket, brought out some

crumpled bills, and counted them off. Mr. Klassen picked them up and put them in the drawer without straightening them. He made change and put three cents on the counter.

"That'll buy half a slice of halva," he said, smiling down at the boy, but the man just picked up the pennies and slid them into his pocket. He lowered the bag of flour onto his hip, picked up the *schmeeaktich*, and started for the door. The boy looked up from the halva, directly at Steven, and smiled. Then he picked up the other sack and followed.

Steven got up and walked to the window. The man was just closing the trunk and the boy was standing beside him, saying something. They separated and got into the car. When the boy said something else, the man leaned over and lashed at him with the back of his hand.

The car pulled away, and when it reached the corner, turned west and headed up into the hills.

"I never saw them around here before," said Steven over his shoulder.

"Paraguayans," said Mr. Klassen. "They say there's a bunch of 'em came back and went to live up in the hills. You don't see them around here a lot. They keep pretty much to themselves." He went back to cutting up his halva.

———

Steven leaned against the plywood wall and looked up into the trees. The leaves were just beginning to turn, and when there was a gust of wind, one or two would float down into the tree house.

There were three of them on Bill's back, who was on his stomach, sprawled across the rough boards, his head over the side. The cottonwoods creaked and moaned against the afternoon breeze. A dog's muffled bark carried up through the branches.

Steven had just finished telling Bill about what happened at the store. Bill hadn't seemed very interested, except to say, "Prugs. All they know how to be is poor. That's what Pa says."

After that he had just rolled over, away from Steven, and stayed that way for a long time. He could be like that.

But now, Bill sat up quickly. "Let's go to the hills," he said.

"What, now?"

"Sure, why not?"

"The wind'll be against us."

"Not on the way back."

"I don't know. It's too far."

"I'll race you down Slide Canyon. We haven't done that since you got your new bike. Maybe now you'll beat me." Bill looked at him, a wide grin on his face.

Two hours later they were standing in a clearing, high above the valley floor, looking out to the east. It had been a tough ride up, but the view today was worth it. The villages below were so many green islands on a blanket of yellow and black.

You could see Rosengart and Blumenfeld, Reinland and Nuehorst. Far off, at the horizon, were the white oil tanks of Gretna. That was almost thirty miles.

To the south, across the line, the arrangement was

different. Instead of large green clusters, there were smaller patches of green, scattered evenly across the plain, each one standing apart.

"Okay, that's enough," said Bill. "Let's go."

"We'll go in a minute." Steven wanted to reward himself a little longer for the hard work they had just completed. It was a familiar exchange—Bill wanting to go, Steven wanting to stay and take things in a little longer.

But Bill's impatience was impossible to stand up to for long. They started back down, coasting recklessly around curves and down steep slopes. They were side by side when they hit Slide Canyon.

Bill pedalled furiously, his head low above the singing tires, handlebars shaking. He pulled slightly ahead of Steven, but then there was a long, straight hill, and Steven caught up quickly.

At the base of the hill was a dirt road, one they had always ignored because of their speed, but now Bill pointed and shouted across at Steven, "Let's try in here." He came upright and stood on the pedals. Steven did the same.

They turned in and headed south down the narrow tracks. Soon they were riding between two ridges, the oak trees thick on either side. Now and then things would open up where a bank of shale had come away from the side of the hill.

At one of the shale hills there were tire marks, and dark patches where the shale had been disturbed. Farmers down in the valley who couldn't afford gravel used it for their driveways and yards. Bill's place was covered with the stuff.

A barbed wire fence ran along one side of the road,

but the grass on the other side was high, and the trees weren't rubbed up at all. Then it thinned out quickly and the road ended on a ridge of bare shale.

They got off their bikes, leaned them on either side of a lone scrub oak, and walked to the end of the ridge. Bill pushed at the shale with his foot and sent a wave of flat grey stones clattering down the steep incline.

"Wanna slide down?"

The slope dropped away evenly for about fifty feet, then narrowed into a channel that disappeared into the trees below.

Bill didn't wait for an answer. He yelled out and jumped, skidding over the shale with his feet tucked under and his arms out wide. It was only a second before he disappeared into the trees. Then it was quiet.

"Bill."

There was no answer.

Steven cupped his hands. "Bill, are you down there?"

Bits of shale still clattered away down the slope.

"Can you hear me?"

There was nothing to do but jump after him. He tried to keep his feet under him, but the speed threw him back and then out of control, the trees on either side a green blur. The air rushing past him was suddenly cold. He hit a large mound of shale that pushed him upright and brought him to a running stop. Bill was waiting for him.

"Hoooooooweee!" yelled Steven.

Bill grinned back at him. "Some ride, eh?"

They stood facing each other, catching their breath, beating the moist fragments of shale from their clothes.

They were beside a shallow creek. The clear water rippled lightly over a bed of clean, fine shale. It was cool and quiet under the canopy of trees.

"This is great!" said Steven, looking around. He leaned over and took up some water with the cup of his hand.

Bill sat down and took off his shoes. "Let's go for a walk," he said, and waded into the water without even testing it.

Steven placed his shoes next to Bill's and followed. He touched one of the large ferns growing out over the creek. "This is like a jungle," he said. "Are you sure we haven't gone over the line?"

"Who cares?" answered Bill, without turning around. "It doesn't matter up here."

When they came around the next bend there was something lying across the creek up ahead of them.

"Look at that," said Steven, splashing up beside Bill.

"It's a bridge," said Bill, scampering over the slippery shale and up onto the embankment. The bridge was made of thin logs, with some rough boards nailed across the top. There was a trail leading away on either side.

They heard a dog bark.

"Somebody lives up there!" said Steven. "Maybe we'd better go back."

"No, it's all right," said Bill. "This way."

It was only a minute before the trail opened up into a clearing. The dog was lying in front of a small, unfinished shack. The corners hadn't been trimmed yet, and the grey boards stuck out here and there at odd lengths.

There were two small squares cut out for windows, and through them they could hear the sound of a baby bawling.

When the dog saw them, he raised himself up and began to bark in earnest. A boy stepped out into the patchy sunshine.

"That's him!" said Steven. "That's the boy from the store."

A girl, maybe seven or eight, appeared behind him. Her tangled hair fell off her shoulders when she leaned out of the doorway. The boy started toward them.

"Stay here," said Bill, and walked ahead.

The two met in the middle of the clearing, and talked with their heads down. Steven couldn't make out what they were saying, but a couple of times the boy raised his head and looked up at him. Then they came over together.

"This is Steven." Bill gestured slightly. "He came, too."

"I saw you in the store," said Steven.

"What store?"

"You know, down in Haskenfeld. Klassen's store."

"Maybe, I don't remember."

"This is Rudy," said Bill. "He's coming with us."

"*Nah yo*," said the boy, glancing over his shoulder. "Let's go."

The little girl ran up and stood beside her brother. "Can I come, too?"

"No, you stay here."

"I wanna go. Please."

"No." Rudy turned on her and she backed off a few feet, but when they started off the little girl followed.

Rudy wheeled and his left hand caught her across the face. She sprawled back, crying.

"I said to stay here," said Rudy. "Now get inside."

He lifted his foot and gave her a thumping kick that made her wail louder. Steven's eyes followed her as she limped, whimpering, back to the house. Rudy turned back to them and smiled. It was the same smile Steven had seen in the store. "Come on," he said. "Let's go."

They walked back down the trail until they got to the bridge. They made their way down into the creek, wading through the cold, shallow water. The dog followed up on the bank, disappearing into the woods now and then.

Steven stopped at a familiar-looking mound of shale. "Isn't this where we came down?" Bill and Rudy shook their heads and kept walking. When Steven caught up, he turned to Rudy and asked, "Where do you go to school?"

"Don't."

"You don't go at all?"

"Nope."

"How come?"

"Don't have to."

"Everybody has to."

"Pa says I can learn everything I need to know from him."

They reached another mound of shale, but this time Steven didn't say anything. It turned out to be the right one, and they clambered up, spaced well apart to let the shale settle. It was tiring, because no matter how far you dug in your heels, the shale would let go and you would slip back almost as far as you had come.

The dog was waiting for them when they got to the top, lying on its side, a little back from the edge, tongue hanging out.

"That was tough," said Steven. "Going down's better."

They sat in a row, looking down at the tops of the trees. Steven got up and called the dog over, sucking air between his puckered lips at short, sharp intervals. The dog raised its head, then cowered up to him, ears back, tail wagging low. He ran his hands through the knotted fur behind his ears and ruffled the shaggy mane.

He had noticed earlier that the dog's eyes did not look right, and now, up close, he saw that there was a thin film over one of them. The dog danced with his front paws and one of them scratched across Steven's bare feet.

"The shoes," he said, looking at Bill. "We forgot them down there."

"I'll go," said Bill. "I wanna slide again anyways." He disappeared as quickly as he had the first time, little rivers of shale trailing after him.

Rudy stood up and looked over at Steven. "He likes you," he said.

"Who?" asked Steven, confused. "You mean Bill?"

"The dog."

"Oh, yeah, I guess so."

Rudy walked up to the dog and grabbed him firmly by one ear. "You like him, don't you, eh fella?" He pulled harder and the dog whimpered. "He's something, this dog. I've got him trained so I can do anything to him. He doesn't care. Here, I'll show you."

He put one hand on either side of the head, resting

his thumbs over the dog's eyes. He smiled up at Steven. "Watch this." Rudy braced himself and forced his thumbs slowly into the eye sockets, until they were completely out of sight.

The dog, his front paws set, barked out sharp shouts of pain, but the boy held on, following the dog's head as it swung from side to side. He pulled his hands back and the dog scuttled out of reach. It stood there, head and tail down, shivering and whimpering quietly. "Bet you can't do that to your dog."

Steven could only move his eyes from the dog, up to the boy, and back to the dog. Rudy turned and walked over to the bikes, still leaning against the scrub oak. Rudy grabbed the handlebars of Steven's new three-speed. It was a bright red next to the faded blue of Bill's old balloon tire.

"That's mine," said Steven. "The red one's mine."

Rudy straddled the crossbar and began to pedal, moving slowly and wobbling his way down the road. Then he got his balance and picked up some speed.

Steven ran behind him, but before he could catch up, Rudy turned awkwardly and headed back toward him. "That's enough," said Steven mildly, but Rudy made a wide loop and rode past him.

Steven turned. "That's enough," he shouted.

The dog got up and ran toward the bike, his tail wagging crazily from side to side. Rudy took one foot off the pedal and kicked viciously at the dog. "Get outa my way, *hund.*"

"That's all," said Steven, as Rudy turned again at the edge of the ridge. He ran up quickly and grabbed the handlebars before the other boy could manoeuvre around him.

The bike stopped so suddenly that Rudy flew over the crossbar and landed heavily on the bare shale. He got up slowly, holding his head.

The two of them stood looking at each other. Steven found himself enjoying a small trickle of blood that ran down Rudy's forehead.

"You don't have to get rough about it," he said. "All I did was take it for a little ride."

Just then Bill rode up and stopped. He looked at Rudy, then at Steven. "What's going on?" he asked.

"Nothing," said Steven, straddling his bike. "I'm going home." He pushed off and started down the road.

He hadn't gone far when Bill pulled up alongside him, holding out a pair of shoes. "Here. You forgot these."

Steven took hold of the shoes and hung them over the handlebars. They rode side by side.

"Aren't you going back?" Steven asked.

"No."

"Good. I don't like him."

"Why not?"

"He doesn't know how to act."

When they got back to the gravel road, they turned east, coasting casually out of the wooded hills and down into the valley. The sun had just set behind them when Bill, without turning, said, "He's my cousin."

Crossing the Line

A steady wind blew out of the west, but down in the shelter of the creek bed, it was calm. The sun shone warmly, and the smell of old, damp clay filled Steven's nostrils. He walked on a crust of dry tiles that cracked under his feet with dull, satisfying snaps. Only a few months ago, meltwater roaring down out of the hills had filled the channel where he walked. Now, in the heat of July, all that remained was a little moisture trapped beneath the surface.

He spotted a mound of fresh, dark clay and squatted down over it. He scattered the tiny, moist balls of mud with a stick, then dug down into the earth beneath. A blue and green claw appeared.

He placed the thin end of the stick between the pincers. When they closed on it, he tugged gently, and pulled the crayfish into the air. Silly creatures, he thought, to actually catch themselves.

He grabbed the tail and the crayfish released the twig. The claws waved in circles, nipping at the air. He held it at eye level for a while, then set it down on a grey tile of clay.

Steven thought of crushing it with his foot, or impaling it on the end of the stick. It would become just another pitiful creature that gave up its life just because he felt like taking it. He watched its slow, clumsy retreat back to the moist hole he had pulled it from, and decided to let it live.

He continued along the winding path of the creek until he found what he was looking for. There, leaning against the bank, was a wooden platform, made up of crude planks. Its square shape had been distorted, and some of the boards hung at loose angles.

They had been floating down the creek on the hastily built raft, pretending to be Tom Sawyer and Huck Finn. Now they stood side by side, each one leaning against a long pole stuck into the hard mud bank, to keep them from going any further. Steven was pointing at something up ahead.

"Let's go," shouted Bill.
"Go where?"
"Over. Let's go over."
"It's too dangerous."
"The water's not that deep. We'll be all right."
"But it's cold. There's still ice in it."
"Come on, Stevie boy, where's your sense of adventure?"

He turned away from the wreckage and climbed the bank. He pushed through the scrub brush that lined the sides of the creek, and struggled through a stand of tall grass that tangled itself around his legs.

Then he was out in the open, leaning against the wind. Young wheat stalks, countless in number, shivered above the hot, black soil. The even rows stretched into the distance until they blended into a smooth, green blanket. Beyond that lay a ridge covered with wild grass, a few shrubs, and an occasional tree. Those lonesome, isolated trees belonged to no one, had been planted by no one, would die without anyone ever noticing.

When he got to the ridge he stopped in front of a steel marker about three feet high. He had examined it many times. There were some numbers on it, and the words "Canada" on one side and "United States of America" on the other.

He scanned the horizon. The nearest farm on the American side was just far enough away to make it seem foreign, out of reach. It was the same on the Canadian side. Few of the Mennonite farmers had built their houses less than a mile north of the border, and so Steven could wander there in relative isolation from the rest of the world—alone, free, unwatched.

He took a few steps onto the ridge and looked up. Under a sky as big as that, his loneliness was complete. He was the only person in the world. He was nothing—and everything. He stood for a long time, motionless. A meadowlark sent sharp, important notes across the wind.

"Let's go."

"Go where?"

"Over. Let's go over."

"We can't."

"Who'll stop us?"

"I just don't think we should, that's all."

"Why not?"

"I—I don't know. It just doesn't seem right. We could get in trouble."

"What are they gonna do to us if they do catch us? Shoot us?"

They stood in silence for a few moments.

"We won't go too far," said Bill. "If we hear or see anything, we'll just high-tail it back over." He began to walk slowly and steadily south.

"I'm not going. You go ahead. I'll wait here."

Bill crossed the ridge and walked into the field on the other side. "I don't feel any different," he shouted back. He walked a few more steps, broke into a run, then stopped and jumped up and down a few times, bringing his feet down hard on the dark soil. "Ground feels the same. Dirt's dirt, I guess." He looked over at Steven, who was standing on the ridge.

"Come on back, Bill. That's enough."

Bill squatted down and rocked on his haunches, a broad smile on his face.

"You got no sense of adventure, Stevie boy, no sense of adventure at all."

A plane came out of the east, flying slowly, lazily along the border, a hundred feet above the ground. He watched it fly over his head and followed it until it reached the hills that lay to the west.

There, a swath had been cut through the trees to mark the line. The liquid shadow of the plane moved up and down over the contour of the slopes, grazing the edges of the trees on either side. Then it was gone.

Perhaps it was a sign.

He was heading up the dirt road that went by Bill's place when Susie, on her way to the barn with a milk pail, spotted him and waved. He should have cut across the field, the way he usually did, but it was too late now. He waved back and stayed on the road.

Two of the older boys, probably John and Peter, were leaning over the front of a car, their heads hidden under the hood. He was glad they were too busy to notice him. They might have waved him over, and that would have meant making awkward conversation, pretending things were still the same.

Mrs. Friesen, her flowered kerchief wrapped tightly around her head, was hanging clothes out on the line. He had never seen her without that kerchief—wasn't sure he'd recognize her if he ever did. Mr. Friesen ambled out of the machine shed, a roll-your-own cigarette dangling from his bottom lip. He walked by two of the younger girls playing on a swing under one of the giant cottonwoods.

As long as Steven could remember, there had been an endless assortment of brothers and sisters at Bill's place. When an older brother left home for a job in town, or a sister married and went to live with her husband, there was always a new brother or sister born to take their place. He wondered if there would be a baby soon, now that Bill was gone.

When he turned into his own driveway a few minutes later, there was no sign of life. Nothing moved in the yard. The buildings seemed asleep under the hot sun. He wanted to be happy, now that he was home, but it was no use.

He found his sister Trudy playing with a kitten in the doorway of the summer kitchen. "Where've you been all day?" She smiled up at him. "I've been waiting for you."

Steven bent down next to her and stroked the kitten.

"I wish you'd let me come along sometimes. I promise not to get tired."

"Sure, but not until you're a little stronger."

"Can we try the bicycle again?"

"Sure, just let me get a drink of water."

"Okay, I'll get the bike." She placed the kitten gently on the ground, pulled herself upright, and disappeared around the side of the house.

Steven walked up the steps and into the cool, dark kitchen. His mother was standing at the counter with her back to him. She turned and looked over her shoulder.

"You were gone a long time," she said.

Steven lifted the ladle from a bucket of cold water and drank deeply. "I went for a walk." He hung the ladle over the side of the bucket and turned to go.

"One of the boys was here asking for you—Peter, I think. A bunch of them were going riding in the hills today." She turned to face him. "You can't spend all your time moping around like this. It's not like Bill was the only friend you ever had." There was frustration on her face, but her voice was tender and pleading.

They stood in silence. He could let it all go now. Maybe then it would be over. Really over. But he knew it could never be that easy.

"Trudy wants to try the bike again," he said flatly.

He turned and walked back out into the summer heat. Trudy was straddling the bicycle, her good leg on the ground, the other one up on the pedal.

"I'm ready."

He grabbed the seat with one hand and the handlebars with the other. "Now remember, pedal as hard as you can, and try to keep your balance." They started out across the yard. He ran beside her, holding the bike upright. When he let go of the handlebars, the bike wobbled awkwardly.

"Keep the handlebars steady. Try to use your own power. Tell me when you want me to let go, okay?"

"Not yet. I'm not ready. I'll tell you when."

They travelled around the yard pole in large circles. "I'm barely holding on," Steven panted. "You're doing great. I'm going to let go now."

"No, not yet. I'm not ready."

"Try to pedal harder, and steer the way I showed you."

He let go for a moment, his hand in position, inches from the seat. The bike lurched to one side. Trudy let out a frightened yell. Steven put his hand back to keep it upright.

"No, please. Stop. I want to stop."

He grabbed the handlebars and brought the bicycle to a complete stop. Trudy put her foot on the ground and he let go, breathing hard. Thin drops of sweat ran down his temples and along the sides of his face.

She had been trying to learn how to ride the bike for most of the summer. It wasn't her fault. The polio had eaten away too much of the muscle in her leg. One arm was smaller, too, but most people didn't notice that.

It would be different if Bill were here. He would say something, do something, to make Trudy understand. He would find a way to make her believe that she could do it. And then, before anyone could stop it from happening, she would be riding the bike on her own, laughing and shouting.

Bill could do things like that.

"We'll try again tomorrow, okay?" Steven said finally.

"Okay." Trudy dismounted and led the bicycle across the yard. She leaned it carefully against the side of the house, then picked up the cat and sat down in the doorway of the porch.

"I'll see you later, okay?" said Steven gently. Trudy smiled and put her face next to the kitten's.

Steven walked past the outbuildings, through a small pasture, and into a wooded area. The largest trees were on the far side, mainly cottonwoods and willows, planted there to protect the apple orchard that grew along the southern exposure. He strolled between two rows of fruit trees, looking up into the branches. Little green apples, countless in number, hung among the leaves.

They lay on their backs under a canopy of pink and white blossoms, the smell of warm earth and nectar in their nostrils. An oriole sang brilliantly, its orange and black colours flitting in and out of sight above them. Bits of powder blue sky showed here and there through the thick branches.

A sudden gust of warm air blew through the trees and then it was snowing—soft, sweet-smelling flakes that nestled in their hair and settled on their upturned faces.

"It's the best time, isn't it?" Steven said.

"The very best," Bill answered.

"If winter came back tomorrow, I wouldn't care."

"Me either."

Steven found himself walking along the creek bed again, as he had so many times that summer. The sound of rushing water behind him made him turn in spite of himself, even though he knew it was only the wind gusting down out of the hills, the way it always did on hot summer afternoons.

Early mornings offered an hour or so of still air, when sounds were true and scents were pure. Late evenings brought a breeze so gentle that only the rustle of leaves, high in the cottonwood trees, gave it away. Those were the calm, quiet times. But the rest of the day belonged to the wind.

He climbed the bank at the usual spot and looked out across the field. At first he thought it must be a mirage. He had been fooled before. The waves of heat rising from the flat fields could distort the shape and size of things. What looked at first like some strange creature could turn out to be nothing more than a clump of weeds left behind by a cultivator.

But as he stared across the field, his eyes fixed on the shimmering image in the distance, he began to make out more details. There was someone on the ridge, someone about his age, dressed in far too many clothes for the hot, dry days of July.

Steven walked slowly, deliberately, expecting at any moment to see the mirage resolve into something ordinary and disappointing. But he was almost at the border now, and still the image quivered before his eyes.

He was running now, hoping to break through whatever it was that would not let him see clearly. He tried to make out the face, but it remained hidden behind a veil of distorted air.

He stopped at the ridge, his arms hanging limply at his sides, his chest heaving, sweat running down the inside of his shirt. He opened his mouth to speak, but no words formed on his lips. A hand reached out toward him. The wind stopped.

———

"Let's go."
"Go where?"
"Over. Let's go over."

———————

Trudy rode in wide circles under the yellow light of the yard pole. Her mother stood in the doorway of the summer kitchen, weeping quietly. "I can't wait to show Steven," yelled Trudy. "He'll be so proud. I'm going to keep riding till he gets home. It's like, all of a sudden, I just knew I could do it."

Egg Shells and Dragon Skin

When Steven heard the gargle of a Volkswagen engine coming up behind him, he didn't have to turn around to know who it was. He headed for the side of the road and waded through the tall grass into the ditch, holding the open bottle of Wynola high. In July, it was the dust, shaking from every dull blade. In January, you could end up waist-deep in the fresh snow. In April, the mud would have you kicking *kjleeta* off your boots for a quarter-mile. Still, it was better than getting run over.

Steven sipped at the Wynola and watched the little blue car drift back and forth across the entire width of the road. Ouhm Kjnaaltz's face was inches from the flat windshield, eyes bulging behind coke-bottle glasses, pale hands perched at the top of the wheel. At least he wasn't leaving tracks in the grass today.

"That man's got no business on the road," Steven's mother would say. "For heaven's sake, Trudy has enough trouble walking down to school as it is, and then he comes along and forces her into the ditch." His mother would say these things over the kitchen table, but it never went any further.

And even if it did get back to Ouhm Kjnaaltz, it wouldn't have made any difference. He was as blind as a beggar in the Bible, but that wasn't going to stop him from driving his car down to the general store whenever he damn well felt like it, which was at least once a day.

Except Sunday. On Sunday the road was safe. You didn't have to worry about Ouhm Kjnaaltz or anyone else for that matter. Dogs could rub their backs into the road kill as long as they liked, then roll over and sleep right in the tracks. Boys could scratch dirty things deep into the road bed with sturdy sticks. Girls could use those same sticks to design enormous games of hopscotch before they went to tell on the boys. On Sunday, the road was a playground.

When Steven got back onto the road, he took his hand off the bottle, tipped it back, and had a long drink.

The dust in his mouth made the Wynola taste just that much better.

At the next crossroads he left the gravel and headed south down the dirt road. He stopped at the bridge and looked down into the creek. The clay bed had dried into an intricate network of grey tiles, each one slightly concave. Dragon skin.

He scrambled down the bank and followed the line of the creek, listening to the scales snap and crunch under his feet. When he came to the wreck of an old raft, he turned up onto the south bank and waded through the brush into the open. He tipped up the bottle to finish it, but the Wynola tasted warm now, and too sweet.

When he brought his head down, his eye caught something in the watery distance. Something at the ridge. His hand tightened around the bottle. A tall figure drifted in and out of the heat waves. He could make out the arms and the legs, walking straight toward him with long, purposeful strides.

When he saw that it was a stranger, he backed off into the bushes that lined the edge of the creek and hunkered down. This man, whose features were becoming clearer with every step, had just walked right over the border as if it weren't there, as if it was just another ridge to cross.

The Pembina Hills lay two miles to the west, with plenty of trees for cover. If someone wanted to sneak over the border, that would be the place to do it.

The stranger was wearing a *paaltz maatz*—the kind an old farmer would wear on his way to the barn in February

—and a heavy grey coat, buttoned all the way down the front. Steven was surprised to see that the face was not tanned and weathered, but pink and tender, the expression a mixture of innocence and alarm—like a child looking for its mother.

The stranger stopped fifty feet away. Steven knew he had been spotted and straightened out of his crouching position. The stranger looked at him for a minute, then lowered his head and continued on his way, passing within a few feet of Steven.

"Good day," hailed Steven.

The stranger gave no sign that he had heard.

"Hello," he tried again, louder this time, but there was no response.

"*Kaust du Dietch raden?*" he tried in German. "*Vooah bast frohm?*" The hobo used his free hand to push aside the bushes at the edge of the creek, manoeuvring a wrinkled paper bag carefully between the branches.

Steven followed him down onto the creek bed and stood off to one side. The stranger looked in one direction, then in the other.

"Where you headed?" Steven asked.

He could tell that this was no ordinary drifter. There was something in his face that cried for help, and Steven wanted to offer it.

"There's a store up that way." He raised his arm, index finger pointing, the others curled around the bottle still in his hand. The stranger turned away, then looked back at the bottle of Wynola, rubbing the back of his hand against his mouth.

Steven held it out and stepped forward. "Here, take it." The stranger put out his hand and took the bottle carefully from Steven. He brought it to his mouth slowly, and took a small sip.

"Go ahead." Steven motioned with his hand. "Finish it." The man drank the remainder in one long swallow and handed the bottle back. "There's a road over this way," said Steven. The stranger looked unsure, then started in the direction indicated.

He was past the wreck and around the bend quickly. Steven followed, but not too close. When the bridge came in sight, the stranger stopped, turned around, and started back the way they had come.

Steven cut him off. "This is it," he said. "This is the road." But the stranger only stepped around him and hurried away.

"Wait," Steven shouted after him. "Wait for me."

———

He finds Trudy on the swing at the back of the house, her withered leg hanging thinly over a patch of hardened dirt. The swing hangs from a chain that grows right into the bark of the black cottonwoods on either side. Every year, another link disappears into each tree.

"Trudy." The words quiver under his breath. "Come with me."

"Where?"

"I've got something to show you."

She gets off the swing, sensing his excitement. "What is it?"

"It's up in the tree house. Come on."

"But you said I can't go there. You said only you and Bill .... " Her voice trails off, " ... could ... "

"It's okay. Let's go. Just don't say anything to Ma."

He leads her around the side of the house where his mother is making soap in the *meea gropen*. She bends over the huge pot with a long wooden stick, stirring in slow, wide circles. The smell of the hot lye stings Steven's nostrils.

"We're just going to the orchard," he says.

"Wait." His mother leans the stick against the side of the summer kitchen and disappears through the doorway. She returns with a small basket. "If there's any plums ready, pick some to bring back. I want to start some jam."

They walk away, trying to be casual.

"And don't go eating those green apples," she calls after them. "You'll get sick."

They leave the yard and cross a clearing into the trees. There are two long rows of fruit trees, then some willow trees, and finally, a big stand of cottonwoods. In one of the tallest cottonwoods, between two large trunks, sits a tree house.

It is there because of Bill. He just came over one day, a hammer in his hand, and said, "Let's build a tree house." They walked among the cottonwoods until Bill pointed up and said, "That one."

Somehow, there were boards and nails and then Bill

was up in the tree, shouting for Steven to hand him up two-by-fours. A frame took shape, then a floor, and by sundown they were up there together, looking out over the orchard.

Trudy looks at the rope ladder. "I don't know if I can get up there."

"Sure you can. Watch." Steven climbs three or four rungs in slow, easy steps, then comes back down. "Just do it like that. I'll come up right behind you. I won't let you fall."

Trudy puts her good leg on the first rung and pulls herself up. The ladder swings away from her and she calls out, but Steven pulls it back and holds it steady. She takes the second rung, then the third, and on until she reaches the opening of the tree house.

"That was fun," she announces.

Steven has followed her through the opening before she notices the stranger sleeping on the floor under an old tarpaulin.

"Who's that?" she whispers, backing against her brother.

"That's what I wanted to show you. It's okay," he answers. "You don't have to whisper. He can't hear you."

"But who is he?" she whispers again.

"I don't know. He came over the border."

"From the States?"

"He just came walking over."

"But how did he get up here?"

"I brought him up. He needs a place to stay. I think he's lost."

Trudy takes a step toward the stranger. "He's too big to be lost, and anyway, why didn't you bring him to the house?"

"I tried to, but he wouldn't go near the place."

"Maybe he's done something bad. How do you know he won't hurt us?"

"He's not like that. He's like...he's like a little boy or something."

"But he's a grownup." She bends over the face, studying it.

"When he wakes up, you'll see."

Trudy sits down against the far wall. "We better tell Ma."

"No! Not yet, anyway. We have to find out more about him."

"What's in there?" Trudy points at a paper bag nestled in the crook of the stranger's arm.

"I don't know, he won't let me near it."

She leans forward, her face inches from the bag. "Smells funny."

"That's just the tarp," Steven answers. "It always smells like that."

Trudy extends her hand slowly, pinches the bag between two fingers, and tugs gently. The bag rustles a little, and the stranger stirs. "Don't," says Steven. "Let him sleep."

Trudy lets go of the bag and pulls her hand away. She sits back against the wall, next to Steven.

They talk quietly to one another, watching the stranger's simple sleep.

They sit in a small triad under the early evening light, watching Sonny eat. They know his name because they have found it printed in large block letters on the inside of his *paaltz maatz*.

When Sonny has finished the last of his meal, Trudy picks up the small purple purse she has brought with her and sets it gently down on the floor in front of her. She turns to Steven, who does the same with a brown drawstring pouch.

Together, they point at the paper bag resting in Sonny's lap. They see the doubt in his eyes, but after some hesitation, he lowers the bag to the floor with the others.

"I'll start," Trudy announces. She opens the purse, removes the contents, and arranges the items neatly in front of her: a plastic hairbrush, a small white diary, two glass figurines, a heart-shaped bottle of perfume, and thirteen lucky pennies.

"Now you take your things out," she says to Steven. He goes into his pouch and brings out a slingshot, three old skeleton keys, a large brown clam shell, and six Blue Ribbon Coffee cards.

"Now it's your turn," Steven says, pointing at the bag in front of Sonny.

Sonny leans forward and unravels the wrinkled folds of the bag. He stretches out the opening and reaches inside. He lifts out a bundle of cloth and holds it in the palm of his large hand. He folds back a layer, brings out a small, white egg, and places it delicately on the plywood floor.

"Dove," Steven says. "That's a dove egg."

The hand goes back into the bundle and presents another egg, this one a dark cream, with brown spots.

"Kildeer," Steven says.

The next one is aqua blue, and a little larger.

"Robin."

When Sonny places the last egg next to the others, there are fifteen in all—each one different, each one perfectly intact.

"Where do you think he got those?" Steven asks the floor.

Trudy leans forward and puts her hand out slowly. Sonny, watching closely, lets her pick one up. She examines it, returns it, and takes another. Steven picks one up and says, "They're empty. All of them. Dried out."

"They're beautiful," Trudy says, smiling up at Sonny. For the first time, he smiles back.

———

On the fourth day they will come with a plate full of *kjieltje* and sausage to find the tree house empty.

"He must be around someplace," Steven will say. "Let's start looking."

They will search the woods and find no trace of Sonny.

"But where would he go, just like that?" Trudy will ask.

They will wander the mile roads and fields all afternoon, with no luck. Finally, they will return to check the tree house one more time, but he will not be there.

"We should tell Ma," Trudy will say. "She'll know what to do."

"Let's wait until morning. Maybe he'll come back."

That evening, sitting at the supper table, they will eat without appetite, wondering whether to save enough for Sonny.

"Well, Ouhm Kjnaaltz finally did it," the father will say around his *shingkin flyshe* and potatoes.

"What's that?" the mother will ask.

"Hit somebody with that stupid little car of his."

"I never heard. Who was it?"

"Nobody knows."

Steven and Trudy will look at each other across the table.

"What do you mean nobody knows? Where did it happen?" Trudy will ask.

"Over at Letkeman's corner. Didn't have a wallet or anything. He was a bum." The father will fill his mouth before speaking again. "Broke both his legs, that's what they said. That's it for Ouhm Kjnaaltz, though, so maybe it's a blessing. After all, it could have been worse. It was only a dirty beggar."

The father will not understand when the son throws his fork across the table and runs out of the house—the mother shouting after him, "*Jung, vawht faylt dee!*"—down

to the corner, the sister close behind on her bike, to find
nothing there but a torn brown paper bag and small
pieces of egg shell scattered and trampled like confetti
along the side of the road.

Special Delivery

The customs agent rested one foot on the running board of the truck and curled his hand over the ledge of the window.

"Name?"

"Solly Hill."

"How's that again?"

"Solly."

"Sally?"

"Not Sally, Solly. Solly Hill."

"Place of birth?"

"Where was I born?" For a split second Solly's brain wouldn't let him have the answer. It was his first time over the border and he was a little nervous about it. "Walterboro," he said, then added, "That's in South Carolina."

The officer looked past him into the empty cab.

"Just you?"

"Unless you count him." Solly nodded in the direction of a small black and white tabby sleeping on the seat next to him. It had come wandering along the loading dock that morning, meowing pitifully.

For some reason, instead of brushing it off the platform with his foot, he had picked it up and thrown it into the cab of the truck.

He smiled and gave the kitten a quick rub behind the ears. The customs agent paid no attention to it.

"Destination?"

"Place called Haskenfeld."

"Purpose of your visit?"

"Making a delivery." He tried to offer the papers, but the agent ignored them.

"What are you carrying?"

Solly pointed out the side of the red truck box with his thumb. The agent pushed off with the raised leg, and turned his neck stiffly. Above "D'antonio Brothers—Wholesalers," the word "FRUIT" had been painted in three-foot letters.

"Fruit?" the agent asked.

Solly nodded.

"Papers."

Solly handed them over.

"How long are you planning to stay?" the agent spoke into the papers.

"No more than a couple of hours, I'd say, one way or the other."

"You can't come back over after sundown, you know that."

Solly hadn't known, but he just nodded.

"Have you ever been convicted of any crime punishable by imprisonment or served any time in a state or federal penitentiary?"

"Huh?" Solly swallowed. "No, sir." He was telling the truth, but somehow it didn't feel that way.

"Are you now or have you ever been under the jurisdiction of a state or federal institution for the mentally or criminally insane or infirm?"

"No, sir."

The agent handed back the papers and stepped off the running board.

Solly waited for a few seconds, then asked, "Can I go now?"

The agent flicked a hand at him.

Solly put the truck in gear and pulled away carefully, wondering whether he'd have to go through the same thing on the way back.

When the card game broke up, Willy came over and sat down in the seat next to Solly. Neither one of them spoke for a couple of miles. Willy brought his glove down out of the rack, put it on, and punched into it with his fist. "Is that all you goin' do?" he asked finally. "Gawk out that window the whole trip?"

"I just like to know where I've been," said Solly.

The windows of the bus were covered with a permanent layer of grime, except for Solly's. At the last stop, while the other players stretched and looked around, he'd been up on a crate with a wet cloth, cleaning it off, same as always.

"I don't know," said Willie. "Lookin' out there just makes me lonesome, kind of."

Solly turned away from the window. They were both new in the league, and Willie seemed a little lost. "I'll tell you a little secret," said Solly. "I've been playing ball for twenty years, and I found out there's only one real home for us, and that's the ball park."

"The ball park," Willy echoed. "Oh, man." He didn't think much of Solly's ideas, but he kept coming back for more.

"It just keeps moving," Solly went on, "that's all. And we move with it."

"That don't make any sense at all."

"No matter where you go, or how strange things feel, you always know how things are laid out there. Take home plate. It's always sixty feet six inches from the pitcher's mound, ain't it?"

Willy stopped punching the glove with his fist. "Any fool knows that."

"Or if you send a pitch into the gap, and go for two, why, you know just where to make your turn so you'll catch a corner of the bag, because it's always in exactly the same place."

"So what?"

"So it's like your own place, you see? You always know where everything is and how things are gonna be."

Willie leaned back and began punching again, but with less force.

When Solly turned back to the window, he caught a glimpse of something in the ditch. He pushed past Willie and ran up to the front of the bus. "Hey, what the hell?" Willie called after him.

"Stop the bus," he told the driver.

"Leave it alone."

"You saw it, too, didn't you?" said Solly.

"I saw nothin," answered the driver.

"I just want to get out and take a look."

"We got miles to cover."

Solly grabbed for the handbrake. The driver pushed him away and swore, then pulled off to the side. Solly kicked open the door and ran back up the road until he found a truck on its side, one wheel still spinning, at the bottom of a shallow ravine.

There was someone in the cab. He smashed through the shattered windshield with his foot and crawled inside. The man was still alive, but bleeding badly. Solly took off his jacket and tied off a bad gash on one leg. Willie came up and crouched to look inside. "Let's get him out of here," said Solly.

Together, they lifted him out and got him to the bus, then to a hospital. Solly wanted to stay and find out whether he was going to be all right, but there wasn't time.

The map called for him to take the first road on his

left after he crossed the border. He'd barely got up to speed when he came to an intersection and turned west onto a gravel road.

There was nothing posted to indicate a town coming up, just a yellow sign in the shape of a diamond that read: CLASS B HIGHWAY. Mr. D'Antonio had told him the place wasn't much more than a store and some empty buildings.

The sun shone harder through the windshield and Solly brought the visor down to block out some of the brightness. A low range of hills lined the horizon.

Solly slowed down. He was coming into a village of some kind. The road, lined with tall shade trees on either side, ran dead straight through, and gave him the feeling he was travelling through a tunnel.

He'd never seen a place laid out this way. The lots were more like big yards, with plenty of outbuildings. And the houses were as big as meeting halls. Solly watched in disbelief as a cow came shambling out through one of the huge doors before he realized they were a house and barn attached to each other.

He caught up to a small boy running along the road. The boy was twirling a stick around inside a rusted steel hoop, rolling it ahead of him. When he stopped and turned to look up at Solly in the truck, the hoop rolled away and disappeared into the grass. Solly waved, but the boy didn't wave back.

The people followed him with their eyes: a woman in a kerchief carrying a pail in each hand, a bearded old man in a black hat sitting in the shade, a girl on a swing between two trees. They watched him in a quiet, careful way—the way folks back home would.

He passed a deserted schoolyard. There was a ball diamond, complete with a backstop made out of tall posts and chicken wire. It had a grass infield, and Solly could make out the bare patch behind third base.

Solly took his spot at third. In between pitches, he looked to see where the other guy had dug in his cleats. You could learn a lot about a player just by looking at those marks.

This guy liked to set up farther off the bag than Solly, and back a ways. That meant he had good range, and an arm. Closer to the bag and in meant he was quick, and had guts.

Next time up, if the game wasn't on the line, Solly would look for something he could turn on and drive down the line, just hard enough to let the third baseman get to it. He wanted to test that arm.

Later, standing on the bag at first, he heard the same loud voice yelling at him from the stands again. Some guy had been on him all night.

He was used to hecklers, but this Joe wouldn't let up. He knew it was exactly the wrong thing to do, but something made him turn and look up into the stands.

He saw a stocky man in a black hat and suspenders, waving a jacket over his head. Solly recognized it immediately as the one he had used that night to stop the bleeding.

After the game the man came down out of the stands and handed Solly the jacket. "Some day, if you don't play anymore, you come see me. I got for you a job, anytime. Anytime. Understand?" Inside the jacket pocket was a hundred dollars and a business card. "Frank D'Antonio — Wholesale Fruit."

As suddenly as he had entered the village, he was out of it. The hills were closer now, and he could make out clearings and other features along the slopes. He spotted some buildings about a half-mile up on the right. One of them had a huge red and white Coca Cola sign on the wall, and some other signs that were too small to make out.

He turned off at the next intersection, and as he got nearer, he could see that the other places were boarded up. Above the windows on one of them, the outline of "JANZEN DRY GOODS" had been left behind where the letters used to be. He swung around and backed the truck up to the store entrance.

Solly stopped to watch the men, walking in groups of three or four, coming out of the mill at the end of the shift. Ever since the league had folded, he'd been trying to settle back into the life of the town— working in the cotton mill with the other men, playing a little ball on the weekends.

But just now, watching them— cotton fibres in their hair and on their whiskers, looking like so many ancient black grandfathers— he had come to a decision. Tonight, he would go home and dig through his baseball trunk to find a small, faded business card.

He was on his way inside when the door opened and he heard a bell tinkle. A little girl stepped across the landing. She looked up at him, her head tilted back, hand on the door latch.

He stepped off to one side and smiled down at her. "Hey, how you doin?" he greeted, walking past her. Her eyes followed him into the dim light of the store. It's him, she thought. It's Prestor John.

Prestor John was a big black man who shared many adventures with a girl about Trudy's age and her older brother. He was very brave, and would do anything to protect them. Whenever there was danger, he always found a way to make everything all right.

In Prestor John's *Treasure*, there was a picture of him walking down the road, carrying the children, one on each shoulder. That picture had stayed in Trudy's mind, and it seemed to her, just now, that he had walked right out of it and into Mr. Klassen's store.

Prestor John disappeared into the store, but in a few seconds he was back out, Mr. Klassen behind him. He walked to the back of the truck, turned the metal handle, and swung the red doors open wide. He jumped up into the dim interior, picking up crates and arranging them while Mr. Klassen watched. The scent of fresh fruit and wood shavings reached Trudy where she stood, off to one side, in the shade of the porch.

Mr. Klassen picked up a steel bar and opened one of the crates. He took out an orange and bit into it, pulling away some of the peel with his teeth and spitting it onto the ground. He squeezed some of the juice into his mouth and swallowed.

Prestor John opened another crate and took out some bananas. Then he pulled the top off a box of apples and Mr. Klassen picked through them a little.

"All right," he said, "bring it in." He went back inside and Prestor John followed with a crate of fruit.

On his third trip he jumped down off the truck with a pineapple in his hand.

"You know what this is?" He was looking right at her, and there was no one else around.

"Of course," she answered. "That's a pineapple."

"You like pineapple?"

"I guess so." She didn't want to tell him that she'd never tasted it.

"You want some?"

"Okay."

Prestor John took out a pocket knife and sliced off the top of the pineapple in one smooth motion. He stuck a big yellow piece on the tip of the blade and held it out to Trudy. A few drops of juice ran down between his fingers and onto the boards of the porch.

"Here," he said.

She took it and bit off a piece, chewing slowly. "That's good," she said, putting the rest into her mouth.

"You want some more?"

She nodded, still chewing. He cut another piece and gave it to her, then pulled an empty crate out of the truck and put it down next to her. "Here, you sit down there and eat."

She sat down on the crate, resting the book she had been carrying on her lap. She saw him looking at her shoe, and the brace attached to it.

He put down the pineapple and carried another crate into the store. When he came back out, he pointed down into her lap.

"What's that book you got there?"

"*Anne of Green Gables.*" She held it up for him to see.
"That a good book?"
"Yes."
"You read a lot of books?"
"I guess so." Actually, she had only started reading a
lot since her father had decided that there were too many
cats.

She watched him take down the double-barreled shot-
gun that hung over the doorway of the summer kitchen. He
opened a yellow and purple box that sat on the ledge and
took out a handful of red shells.

Her mother came and stood on the landing beside her,
but she didn't say anything. Her father slid a shell into each
barrel and snapped them into place with a snug click.

"Too many cats," he said, and stepped through the
doorway.

It wasn't until after the first shot that Trudy understood
what was going on. "Where's Butterscotch?" she said in a high
voice. Her mother's hands tightened around her shoulders. She
tried to squirm out from under them, but her mother pulled her
closer, wrapping her arms around Trudy's chest.

"You can't," said her mother. "It's too dangerous."
There was another gun blast, and at the same time, a short,
wild scream. Trudy twisted around to look into her mother's
face. She could only get enough breath to say, "You have to
stop him."

The gun sounded again, then two more times. When it
was over there were muffled voices in the yard, and then Ste-
ven came in to pick up the spade from the coal bin.

David H. Elias

"Butterscotch?" said Trudy.
Steven nodded quickly, then stepped out again.

"I don't read much but the Bible myself," said Solly.

Trudy's mother came out of the store with a bag of groceries in one hand. "Come on," she said. "Let's go." She looked up at Prestor John, then down at the yellow chunk of pineapple in Trudy's hand. "Did you say thank you?" she asked.

Before Trudy could answer, she turned back to Prestor John and said, "I hope she's not being a bother."

"Bother? Why not at all, ma'am." His smile was so big. "Would you care to try a piece, ma'am?" He cut off another piece and held it out to Trudy's mother. It glistened yellow in the sun.

The way he was acting made Trudy think of the Wadkins Man. Whenever he came by, he always opened his giant black suitcase up on the kitchen table, but not before asking, in a voice like Prestor John's, "Ma'am, would it be all right to set my case down on your fine kitchen table for a few moments?" Only a few men ever treated her mother that way. The preacher was another one. If her mother was talking to him, he'd looked right into her eyes and nod like he was really listening hard. He'd let her finish everything she wanted to say, and then talk carefully, in a smooth low voice, like he'd chosen each word just for her.

The other man who did that was the customs officer. When they came back from shopping at the J. C. Penny in Walhalla, wearing new clothes underneath their old

62

ones, secrets stuffed between the seats, he would lean into the window with a big smile (but not as big as Prestor John's), his hand resting on the ledge of the rolled-down window, and say something that made her mother laugh. It happened every time. How could he think of something funny to say every single time?

"Thank you," said her mother, taking the pineapple and biting into it. Prestor John folded his knife and disappeared around the front of the truck. When he came back he was cradling a half-grown kitten in his arms.

"I found it this morning," he said, "and I don't quite know what to do with it. I was wondering, ma'am, if your little girl here might be interested in having it?"

He held the cat, draped across his dark hands, out to Trudy.

Some Bottles are Easy

———

The laughter that came up through the ceiling brought Steven abruptly out of his sleep. He dressed quickly and hurried downstairs. He could see Trudy through the doorway of the kitchen, riding up and down on a long, black leg.

When he walked in, the leg came to rest and a deep voice said, "Who's that? Steven? Is that you? Come. Let your Uncle Abe get a hold on you." Steven stepped forward and a large hand reached out, grasped his shoulder, and pulled him closer.

Blond eyebrows came out from behind the dark glasses. "Are you sure you're not standing on a milk stool, *jung*? Martha," the voice shouted. "Look how tall your boy is getting. *Vaou sheent it, jung?*" (How does it shine, my boy?) The words formed around a grin of solid teeth.

"*Fawn bowven*," (from up there) Steven answered. It had been more than two years since the last visit, but his Uncle Abe had not forgotten. Ever since he could remember, they had exchanged that same, silly greeting.

His mother brought a pot of coffee and a cup over to the table. "Here," she said louder than necessary, "have a cup of coffee." Steven moved around the table and sat down across from his uncle.

Uncle Abe sniffed the air as his mother poured, then felt carefully for the rim of the cup and took a noisy sip. "Aaahhhh," he sighed, "you always did make a good coffee, Martha." He took another sip.

"How long are you here for?" asked Steven's mother.

"Just a couple of days. They won't let me stay away from my work for too long. It's not every man that can staple together a cardboard box as fast as me." He laughed in that reckless way of his.

Steven sat and watched his uncle drink the coffee. You could look at him as long as you liked and never feel like you were being rude. It was one of the things he liked best about him. You could study his face, all the expressions, all the changes. Other people would turn you away with their eyes, but not Uncle Abe.

Steven went over to the counter and poured a glass of water. He looked out of the window and saw his father coming across the yard toward the house with the same serious steps that carried him wherever he went.

"Dad's coming in," he said, trying to sound casual. When the latch clicked out in the porch his mother stiffened. Uncle Abe put down his cup just as the door opened. His father stopped abruptly, looked sternly at his mother, then walked ahead quickly.

"Isaac, is that you?" greeted Uncle Abe.

Without breaking stride his father said, "Good day," and hurried through the kitchen, leaving small chips of dried manure on the floor behind him.

Uncle Abe turned his head to follow the footsteps. "How goes the farming?" he called out. But there was no reply.

Steven's mother turned to busy herself at the counter. The kitchen clock ticked loudly. Uncle Abe took up his coffee, drank what was left in several large swallows, and brought the cup down with a smart knock. "Come on, *jung*," he said, "we're going to the store."

Steven got up eagerly and grabbed the cane that lay across an empty chair. "Here," he said, bringing the curved end into his uncle's outstretched hand. "I'll get my shoes on."

His uncle put one huge hand on Trudy's shoulder and said quietly, "We'll take another walk when I get back, just you and me." The walk to the store was still more than she could manage. The polio had taken too much of the muscle in her leg.

Out on the road Steven walked beside his uncle,

eyes shut tight. He was trying to imitate the feeling his uncle must be having. He brought his hands up over his eyes to block out more of the sun. He was still seeing pink, and he knew that wasn't right, because he had asked once, "What colour do you see?"

"Colour?"

"Behind your eyes. What colour is it? I always see pink when I shut my eyes tight."

"I don't see any colour."

"You mean it's black?"

"It's not black either. It's just nothing."

His uncle had been blinded a long time ago, in the war. He never talked about it, but Steven knew it had something to do with a big explosion. "Pa says it's your punishment for going in the first place," Trudy had once blurted out before Steven could stop her. But Uncle Abe had just laughed in that big way of his.

He could gauge where the side of the road was from the rustle of the grass whenever he got over too far. He felt a little off balance, and it was hard to keep up with the big strides of his uncle. Then he stepped and the ground wasn't there to meet him. He stumbled forward, fell, and rolled noisily through the tall grass into the ditch.

"What was that?" asked his uncle, stopping.

"It's me," said Steven, getting up quickly. "I found a drink bottle." He hurried back onto the road. "They're two cents now, you know." He looked back and saw that it was a gopher hole he had stepped into.

"Let's see it," said his uncle.

"See what?" asked Steven, picking a burr off his pants.

"The bottle you found. I'll tell you what kind it is."

"Oh, it was chipped so I left it."

When they were on their way again, Uncle Abe lifted his cane and pointed straight ahead. "I sure wish I could see those hills. I can feel them out there."

The blue Pembina Hills shimmered above the flat prairie fields that lay to the west.

"Tell me, do they look close today, or far?"

"Close," Steven lied. It was the answer his uncle would want to hear.

They had made the turn and were heading north when Uncle Abe pulled a white envelope from his pocket and handed it to Steven. "Can you read that?" he asked.

Steven took the envelope and read out loud, "Miss Matilda Nickel. Haskenfeld, Manitoba." The words had been printed in big block letters that looked as if they had been made by someone in first grade.

"I wrote it on the train coming out here," said his uncle. "It took me a long time. I want you to give that to her when you go to school on Monday."

Miss Nickel was the new schoolteacher. Steven liked her very much. She wasn't anything like the other teachers they had had. For one thing, she didn't act like a teacher. She laughed far too often.

For another, she smoked. They had seen her one day, coming out of the girls' outhouse, smoke still escaping from between her lips. He had sent Trudy in, and she had discovered a cigarette still glowing down in the hole. They decided not to tell anyone because they liked her. And besides, she was already in trouble with the inspector.

It was always tense when he came, but the last time had been worse than ever. After watching the lesson for a few minutes, he had called Miss Nickel to the back of the room and whispered something to her. Steven had been able to make out the words "proper attire." He had turned around in time to see Miss Nickel, her neck and face crimson, her chest heaving, doing up the top button of her blouse. The inspector had walked out briskly, without even saying good-bye to the students.

But there was something else that made her different. Usually the teachers were from far away. They were people that nobody knew. They would stay for a year or two and then a new one would come to take their place.

But Miss Nickel had grown up in Haskenfeld, just like everyone else. That was the funny part. For someone who was just like them, she was more different than anybody he knew, except maybe his uncle.

When they got to the store, Uncle Abe said, "Let's have a drink," and led the way over to the cooler. It was quiet and they could hear Mr. Klassen sorting mail in the post office at the back of the store. His uncle felt for the handle on the big chrome lid, then asked, "What kind do you want?"

"Orange Crush," Steven answered. His uncle ran a hand lightly over the bottles, playing his fingers around them, until they tightened around one of the necks. The water made a hollow plop when he pulled the bottle free. It was Orange Crush.

Steven reached for the cloth that always lay on the other lid and wiped the bottle down. The cloth was still dry, but it promised to be a hot day, and by sundown, it would be soaking wet.

His uncle reached in and brought out another bottle. "Uptown," he said. "It's an easy one, with that long neck."

Steven handed him the rag. "The ones that give me trouble are Pepsi and 7-Up. But if you feel the little lumps of glass then you know it's Pepsi." He felt for the opener and inserted the green bottle. There was a hiss, and the cap clattered down into the holding tray.

Steven did the same, his eyes closed. They sat down on the wooden crates that were always there, tilted their bottles back, and drank.

"I'll tell you a story now," said his uncle, "but I have to warn you." Steven liked it already. He had been hoping for a story about the war. His uncle leaned forward, "It's about a girl." Steven should have known it wouldn't be about guns or fighting. It never was.

"This was in Italy. I bet you've never seen an Italian girl, hey? She wasn't like the girls around here. She had big, dark eyes, and when she drank wine, those eyes were full of fire.

"One night she took me to a dance hall—yes," he whispered mockingly into the air, "a dance hall. It had a wooden floor that smelled just like this." He tapped the floor with his cane. Steven took a deep breath, picking up the musty scent of oil. "Anyway, it was hot. We were laughing and drinking, but she kept wanting to dance. I said no, but she kept asking, pulling my arm, trying to drag me onto the floor. Finally, I told her, 'I don't know how to dance.' She just laughed, like I was making a joke.

I said, 'No, really, I never learned how.' She thought I was mocking her. I said, 'Where I come from we are taught that it is sinful.' I felt funny saying that."

His uncle was talking more to himself than to Steven, but now he straightened up and continued in a louder voice. "Anyway, that night she taught me how to dance. I danced with women, old and young, fat and thin. I danced with men. I danced until they pulled me off the floor. It was just about the best night of my life."

He swallowed the last of his drink. "I'm only telling you this to teach you a lesson." He leaned forward, his face serious. "And that lesson is: Let there be dancing!" He got up and threw his arms over his head, stomping around in circles, then stopped abruptly. "Let's go," he said, putting down the bottle on the cooler, and added, "Don't forget about the letter."

On Monday Steven waited until after school before he walked quickly to the front of the room and stood at Miss Nickel's desk. She looked at him and asked, "And what can I do for you, young man?" She was the only one who ever called him that, and it made him feel good every time she said it.

"This is for you." He held out the envelope. For a split second he had the crazy notion that the letter was from him, and that it told his secret feelings for her. It was really a very difficult thing his uncle had asked him to do.

Miss Nickel smiled and took the envelope, but her face became serious when she turned the writing toward her. "What's this?" she asked. "Who's it from?"

"I'm not allowed to say." He wasn't sure if that was true, but he thought it was best to say so. She pulled back one of the drawers and brought out a pair of scissors. She cut across the envelope, pulled out a piece of paper, and unfolded it. She started to read, but then looked up and said, "Thank you, Steven. You can go now."

When he got home, his uncle was waiting for him under the cottonwoods in front of the house.

"Did you give it to her?"

"Yes. After school."

"Good. Did she read it?"

"I guess so."

"You're not sure?"

"I didn't wait."

"Did she say anything?"

"I told you, I didn't wait." He was a little annoyed at all the questions. "I'm going in," he said.

"Wait. After supper I want you to take me to the orchard."

Steven didn't reply.

"Steven, did you hear me?"

"Yes. After supper."

The orchard was set well back from the rest of the yard, and separated from it by a small plot of open land. There were apple, plum, and cherry trees, all in bloom. When they got into the trees, his uncle said, "Smells good, doesn't it?"

They stood under a canopy of white apple blossoms. "I'll tell you a little secret," he went on. "If you want to impress a girl, bring her here. It's a very romantic place."

Then he added, "Go on now. I want to be alone for awhile. Come back in an hour."

Steven left the way he had come, but instead of going back to the yard, he circled around and went up into the tree house that was nestled in one of the large cottonwoods set back from the orchard. It wasn't like he was spying, it was just that he wanted to make sure that his uncle was all right.

He climbed the rope ladder and pulled it up after him. Sheets of plywood walled in the platform on three sides, and another piece lay across the top to form a partial roof.

For a while he sat under the roof, leaning against the wall. Then he went to the edge and dangled his feet over the side. Finally he lay down, hands behind his head, looking up into the trees. The sky showed blue through the new leaves, and the high branches swayed in the wind, rocking the tree house gently.

He thought about his uncle dancing with the Italian woman. He imagined himself dancing with Miss Nickel, moving her expertly around the floor in endless circles. The rhythmic motion of the platform made him drowsy, and he felt himself drifting off.

———

There were voices down below, speaking *Plaut Dietch*. The pleasing aroma of tobacco smoke wafted up through the trees. "I thought it was very foolish of you." It was Miss

Nickel's voice. "For years I lived with a terrible guilt that somehow, I was responsible."

"You know the funniest part?" he heard his uncle say. "I turned out to be a pretty good soldier. Me, a Mennonite. It took me a long time to figure out why, but now I understand. It was because I had the two qualities that a soldier needs most: discipline, and self-denial. We are used to living that way." They both laughed.

Steven rolled over carefully and peeked over the edge. They were almost directly below him. Miss Nickel was drinking from a large bottle. "Here," she said, handing it over. "You have the rest."

"The worst part was coming back here," said his uncle, taking the bottle, "and being treated like an outcast. Silence is what they use against me. You know what a powerful weapon that is." He drank from the bottle. "Sometimes I think it would have been better to be killed instead of just blinded."

"But what were you trying to prove? Going off to fight like that?"

"You ask me what I'm trying to prove. What about you? Coming back here to teach. Here, of all places? If you think you can change anything, you're as blind as I am. For you and me, it's enough that we've learned to survive."

"You're right. We're both fools."

"Perhaps two fools can find a way to survive together."

"Listen to me." She turned to face him. "You and I, we've carried our loneliness for so long that it's become our freedom. Together, we'd only end up taking the very thing we've learned to cherish away from each other—without trying to, without meaning to."

"You are too wise, Tillie Nickel."

"Don't call me that. I'm Matilda now."

They stood face to face. She with her legs tight together, hands at her side; he, leaning against a tree, head down. He brought the cane down on a dried twig and it snapped in two.

She reached out her arms and placed them on his. He pulled her close, then leaned forward to kiss her. One hand came up and began undoing the buttons of her blouse.

Steven rolled over. He didn't want to see anymore. He wanted to run away, but there was no way out. He put his hands over his ears, but still he could hear everything.

"No," he heard her say. "Stop."

"But why? We both want to."

"It wouldn't be me—now—the way I really am. Can't you see that?"

"What do you mean?"

"I've changed. The woman you knew back then is gone. She's the one you want to make love to."

"That's ridiculous."

"Is it?"

"It's not fair, what you're doing."

"I know. I'm sorry. I've had too much wine. I'm going now." There was a short silence. From farther away Steven heard her say, "Good-bye, Abe. Let's not do this to each other anymore, okay?"

"Discipline and self-denial," his uncle shouted.

After that it was quiet for a long time, and Steven finally rolled over to see what was happening. His uncle was sitting some distance away, across a tree branch, hands resting on his cane. Miss Nickel was nowhere in sight.

Steven made his way down, quietly circling around so that he would be coming from the right direction, and announced himself by scuffing his feet over the ground.

They walked back to the yard in silence. Steven thought about a lot of things. He thought about how Miss Nickel wouldn't be the teacher for much longer. He thought about how his Uncle Abe would be leaving for B.C. in a day or two.

And then he thought how much he missed them both already.

On the Shore of an Ancient Sea

They sat on the porch steps and watched the chase. The dog, tongue hanging to one side, eyes in a smile, stayed just close enough to be menacing. The sprinting chicken squawked and threw its head from side to side. The dog put on a sudden burst of speed and the bird leapt into the air, wings thrashing, in a desperate attempt at flight, then veered sharply to one side.

Instead of following, the dog ran straight ahead toward the house, as if it had been heading that way all
along. It slowed to a walk and lay down in the shade of
the porch, panting away the heat, while the chicken
stood, in stupid exhaustion, in the middle of the yard.

"Pa wouldn't like it if he saw her doing that," said
Trudy.

"Well he isn't here to see it," answered Steven. "And
besides, it keeps them away from the house."

"I've never seen her do that before," said Trudy. "I
wonder what's got into her."

"She's just playing. There's no harm in it."

"It's this place. It's making her wild."

"She's fine. She's just having a little fun."

Trudy called to the dog, "Sandy, come here girl,
come on." The dog climbed the steps and lay down next
to her with its head resting in her lap. "You're a bad dog,"
she said, smoothing the fur along the length of its back.
"Yes you are—a bad dog."

Steven ran his eyes along the edge of the forest that
surrounded the farm. The late evening sun cast shadows
through the spruce trees and made the woods seem
thicker. Somehow, darkness seemed to come differently
to this place. Maybe it was just that there were no cottonwoods to reflect the last rays of sunlight high in their
branches.

Only a few weeks ago, looking through the back
window of the car, they had watched the Pembina Hills
thin out to a line, then disappear into the horizon; had
seen the landscape change from wide green fields, thick

with wheat, to timber and rock, where the farms seemed an intrusion on the forest.

It was onto the driveway of such a farm that they had turned, finally, their worst fears realized at the sight of the small, ugly house, the meagre outbuildings, and the neglected, rock-infested fields beyond. And so they sat, now, in the twilight, waiting to be called in for supper, but mostly waiting for the strangeness of everything to soften a little.

When their mother finally called them, they sat down at the table and bowed their heads in a silent grace. Trudy was the last to raise hers up again. She looked over at her mother. "When is Daddy coming home?"

"There's been some trouble with the truck. He won't be back until tomorrow night." Steven's mother got up quickly, went to the kitchen counter, and returned with a pot.

His father had made one last trip back to Haskenfeld for the rest of the machinery. Steven had hoped he might be needed, but on the way home from school yesterday, the bus had passed his father going in the opposite direction with the truck.

"I helped with the chores tonight," said Trudy.

Steven nodded in agreement when his mother looked at him. "She's getting stronger, Ma," he said. "She really is." He didn't tell her that Trudy had been unable to carry the small pail of chop without stopping every few feet to rest, or about the pain in her face when she fell, trying to empty the pail into the trough.

They talked all through the meal, so that there was hardly a crack in the silence. But by the time they had cleared the dishes, they were running out of things to say. It was through just such a crack that the first cry came out of the darkness and into the pale light of the kitchen. It rose, high and slender, freezing them where they stood.

They listened as another voice joined in, then another, until the wailing was a chorus, rising and falling in waves of unnatural harmony. Every night it was the same. The relentless howling, long into the night, into their sleep.

"They're right next to the house," said Trudy quietly, her hand still on the dish she had set on the counter. "They've never been this close before."

"It just sounds that way," said Steven, sensing the fear in his sister's voice. "They're way out in the woods." Still, they did seem closer than he remembered on other nights.

He pushed back his chair and went out through the kitchen door. He walked through the porch and stood out on the landing. The dog sat at the edge of the steps, ears erect, hackles up. Low growls rumbled out of its chest, but in between, faint whimpers escaped.

"Why don't you go and chase them?" he said to the dog. "Chase them the hell on out of here." He went into the porch and pulled a rifle off the rack, loaded a shell into the chamber, and stepped back outside. His breath came in thin clouds under the porch light. He pointed the barrel up into a starry sky and pulled the trigger. The percussion crashed through the crisp autumn air and echoed into the surrounding woods. The dog shook its haunches and crouched into a cower, ears and tail flat, then disappeared in a low belly run down the steps and around the corner.

The howling stopped. "That settled 'em down," said Steven out loud. He lifted the gun up onto the rack and went back into the house, but before he had pulled his chair back up to the table, a low, tentative moan sounded. And by the time he ran out to fire off another shell, it had risen to a cry of high defiance.

———————

Steven was coming in from morning chores when he met Trudy on the steps.

"Where's Sandy?" she said.

"I thought she was with you."

"You mean you haven't seen her either?"

"Not this morning," he answered.

"You mean she wasn't here at all?"

"Don't worry, she'll turn up. Probably out in the woods chasing squirrels. She's still not used to them."

Trudy clumped down the steps, went out into the yard, and called loudly, "Sandy, Sandy, come here girl, come on Sandy." But the dog was nowhere in sight.

When they got off the school bus that evening, Sandy was still not there to greet them. Trudy hurried awkwardly up the long driveway and into the yard. All through chores she wandered in and out of the yard and along the edge of the woods, calling.

They were sitting on the steps before supper, the way they did every night, when the dog appeared at the far end of the clearing. It emerged from the woods, sat on its haunches for a few moments, as if sniffing the air, then trotted toward them. Trudy got up and called to it.

The dog picked up speed as it neared the yard, but instead of coming up to Trudy, it burst, sleek and low, into the flock of chickens that had gathered in the evening light near the coop.

They exploded in a chaos of wings and legs. The dog singled one out, and before it had gone ten yards, jumped—head turned sideways—and snapped the outstretched neck of the bird between it jaws. The chicken collapsed and the dog released its grip, pushing off with its front paws. The bird thrashed crazily, its head pivoting at unnatural angles around a broken neck. One outstretched wing beat the dry ground, twisting the bird in a tight circle of dust and feathers.

The dog bounded along the edge of the turmoil, barking, until the wings came to rest. Then it raced toward the coop, and in a matter of seconds another bird was left twitching on the ground.

Trudy stood in the middle of the yard screaming at the dog to stop. Steven tried to scare it off, throwing rocks and yelling, but the dog ignored them both and went after another bird. Steven ran to the porch. By the time he got back, a third bird was dead. But instead of going after another bird, the dog turned away from the coop and headed directly for Trudy. She put out her arms and called to the dog. "Come here, girl." The dog charged toward her, teeth bared, ears pinned back.

Steven fired. The shot sent the dog stumbling sideways until its front feet buckled and it fell, slowly, at

Trudy's feet. He ran up beside her where she knelt, at the edge of a cherry-black pool forming under the dog's chest. She stroked the raised head gently, until it came to rest in the dirt, the jaw open and awkward.

Trudy looked up at Steven.

"I thought..." He started again. "She was..." He wanted to tell her why he'd done it, but her eyes wouldn't let him. He turned away quickly and walked in the direction of the toolshed.

His mother hurried around the corner of the house and ran up beside Trudy, who was still sitting next to the dog, stroking its head with her small hand.

She knelt next to Trudy for a moment, then said, "Come away," and took her up by the shoulders.

"It was the wolves," said Trudy.

"Let's go inside," said her mother. She turned Trudy away from the dog and they started for the house.

"I hate them," said Trudy, limping away.

———

Steven gathered the dog in his arms and laid it across the wheelbarrow, then headed into the clearing beyond the yard. He would have preferred to bury the dog in the woods, but darkness was falling fast. He stopped near the edge of the clearing and began to dig. The blade cut easily into the sandy soil. He lifted out a load of dirt and threw it to one side. It landed with a hollow thump and broke into a dozen small grey clumps. He was surprised at how easily the dirt gave in to his shovel. Back home, the rich soil would not have allowed itself to be disturbed so easily.

In a few minutes he had a hole three feet across and two feet deep. It was almost too easy. Somehow, he had wanted this to be more difficult. Then he hit something hard. He cleared away the sand to reveal a bed of flat, tightly packed stones, each about the size of his hand.

He stabbed at them with the spade. The hollow sound told him that it was only a thin layer, but the stones would not be pried apart. He couldn't seem to wedge enough of the blade between them to get any leverage. He finally resorted to swinging the spade like an axe, smashing it down onto the hard layer. Half an hour later he was still hacking away, swearing at the stones as they sparked under the battered edge of the spade. With every swing he could feel them give way, and yet he could not break through.

His mother called out through the thin autumn air, but he didn't answer, only stopped to rest under a huge moon that had risen over the tree line. His clothes were wet with perspiration, in spite of the coolness of the evening air.

Then, in one blow, punctuated by a curse, the stones crumbled into a loose mass. He cleared them away and found the earth beneath shining back at him under the moonlight. He lifted out spade after spade of the purest, whitest sand he had ever seen.

He jumped into the hole, digging tirelessly, the smell of the sand cold and damp in his nostrils. Each spadeful seemed easier than the one before. He widened the hole, smashing away more and more of the hard layer, which crumbled easily now that he had broken through, then clearing it away to reveal more perfect sand. He dug until his arms gave out, until they would no longer obey his will. The spade fell away from his hands and he found himself waist deep in a great glowing circle made of its own light.

He fell to his knees, plunging his hands in—letting the exquisite powder swallow them—bringing up handfuls of sand and letting it slip slowly through his outstretched fingers. He looked up at the sky and became aware of the sudden, crushing stillness.

For the first time in his life, he felt the pull of the moon.

At the edge of the circle, eyes shone.

A Hand to Hold

———

The pads of Steven's feet slapped gently against the cold surface of the kitchen floor. He was careful to avoid the cracks in the linoleum. If you stepped on them they closed up and pinched your skin. There were better ways to start your day.

The screen door offered familiar resistance as he pushed against it and stepped onto the porch of the farmhouse. He stood with his fingers in the front pockets of his jeans, squinting under the fresh sunlight. A flock of sparrows fed noisily near one of the grain bins. Their harsh chatter annoyed him. He wanted to hear the song of a mourning dove, or an oriole. Sparrows were so ordinary.

Back in the kitchen, the air was stale. He made room at the cluttered table and shook some cereal into a bowl. He stood over it for several seconds, then poured the cereal back into the box and stacked the bowl on top of the other dirty dishes. He would eat porridge without milk, but not dry cereal.

A pot of coffee simmered on the stove. He poured a little into a cup, sipped gingerly at it, then spit it back into the cup. It was even more vile than he had expected.

Footsteps sounded heavily on the porch. His father came in, walked over to the stove, and poured a cup of coffee. He walked over to the table with the cup in his hand and sat down. He shoved aside some dishes, rested an elbow in the space he had created, and raised the cup to his lips.

"Don't drink it," Steven warned. "It's awful."

His father sipped noisily at the rancid coffee. "We're going out to Gladstone today," he said, his eyes fixed on the unused bowl Steven had left. "There's some barley we can take in. I'll take the pickup and you can follow in the truck."

His father, cup in hand, turned to look out through the kitchen window. His expression reminded Steven of a man walking headlong into a blinding snowstorm. "There'll be people snooping around here pretty soon," he said.

"They're after this place now. Let 'em take it. It's not worth sweating over anyway."

The highway started from a point on the horizon and widened out slowly until it ran directly under the wheels of the truck. Fields lay perfectly flat on either side. Steven's arm ached from holding the transistor radio next to his ear, but it was the only way he could hear over the deafening roar inside the cab of the old truck. Buck Owens was singing "Tiger By The Tail," and Steven was singing along.

"IIII've - - - gawwwt - - aaaa - tiger by the tail it's plain to seeeeeee, Ana wonbe muchwen yugithruuuu with meee."

A car pulled out to pass and he saw that it was a young woman driving. When she pulled even with him, he looked down into the car, hoping to see exposed thighs under a short skirt. But all he saw was a grey pair of slacks. It was always like that.

Steven could see his father's head through the back of the pickup truck up ahead. Every few minutes it would move forward, stay there for a few seconds, then move back. His father was always playing with the radio. Steven wondered just what it was he was trying to find. He knew it wasn't country music.

When they turned off the highway and onto the gravel road, Steven had to put the radio down. He couldn't control the old truck with one hand any longer. Besides, with the stones pounding against the undercarriage, the noise inside the cab was just too much. He sang to himself in spite of the din. *"Heartaches byyy the numberrrrrr – troubles by the scorrrrre – evrydayyoulovemeless – eachdaylloveyoumorrrrre."*

The pickup was throwing up a nasty trail of dust. There was no sense in staying right on his father's tail. He let the distance between them widen.

He had all but lost sight of the pickup when he noticed someone standing in the driveway of a farmyard up ahead. He saw that it was a girl and slowed down a little. She was wearing a blue dress, and her dark blond hair reached down to her shoulders. She was about his age, and even from a distance he could see that she was pretty.

Her attention seemed to be focused on the far side of the road, and when Steven took a closer look he noticed a cat bounding through the tall grass in the ditch. It was making its way up the steep slope toward the road, heading for the girl and the farmyard.

The girl cupped her hands to her mouth and shouted something, then turned in Steven's direction. When she brought her hands away from her face, he was shocked to see how contorted it had become. It wasn't pretty anymore.

The cat took no notice of the truck and started across the road. He was sure to hit it. Normally, he didn't concern himself with small animals on the road. He couldn't be bothered with a creature that was stupid enough to let itself get run over. But now he gripped the wheel firmly and pushed down hard on the brake pedal. The rear wheels locked and the truck slid sideways. He turned into the skid, released the brakes just long enough to straighten out, then pushed down again. The truck came to a stop just beyond the driveway.

He knew he had missed the cat. There was always

that telltale bump—not like a rock or a piece of wood—when something alive went under the wheels.

He got out of the cab and walked back toward the girl. She was cradling the cat in her arms, rubbing its head against her blue dress where it covered her small breasts. She looked up at him. There was no sign of the pain he had seen just seconds before. Instead, she smiled warmly.

"Is he okay?" asked Steven, even though he could see clearly that the cat was unharmed. He was close enough to reach out and touch it, but he didn't.

"She," said the girl, still smiling at him. "It's a female. She's fine."

"I'm glad," he said. He was glad. He really was glad.

"Are you all right?" she asked.

"Yeah, sure. I'm okay." He was surprised at her question.

They were silent for a moment. "Thanks," he said. "For asking, I mean." That was stupid. He shouldn't have said anything.

A man walked up the driveway toward them. He was wearing patched overalls and carrying a grease gun in one hand. "What's going on here?" he asked, but not in an angry way.

"Penny was crossing the road," answered the girl, "and he had to stop for her, that's all."

The man looked at the truck, then back at Steven.

"Everything's all right, Daddy, really," she said, then to Steven, "Thanks for stopping."

"Yeah," said her father, "'preciate it." He pulled a rag out of his pocket and wiped the grease gun with it. "Hope we didn't cause you too much trouble."

"No trouble at all, sir," said Steven.

"Is the truck okay?" the man asked.

"The truck's fine," Steven answered. He didn't give a damn about the truck. He wanted to talk to the girl some more, but her father just stood there, looking at him.

"Well, I'd better be going," said Steven. "Bye."

"Good-bye," said the girl, "and thank you again."

On his way back to the truck he heard her the man say, "Doesn't look old enough to drive."

He got back into the truck and started down the road. He could see the girl in the rear view mirror, the cat still in her arms, walking slowly back down the driveway. Her father was behind her, swinging the grease gun back and forth. The skirt of her blue dress billowed in the breeze and brushed against the tip of the nozzle.

When he arrived at the farm, his father was standing on the wheel of the grain auger, working on the engine.

"What the hell happened to you?" his father asked.

"I had to stop."

"What for? Is there something wrong with the truck?"

"I thought it might be overheating, so I stopped to check the water." Steven looked down at the wheel his father was standing on.

"Get the socket set out of the truck," said his father, and turned his attention back to the engine.

The place looked even more desolate than Steven remembered. The windows of the empty farmhouse had been shattered and long grass covered most of the yard. Other than the grain auger, there was no machinery in sight.

When his father had finished, they pushed the auger

into one of the bins and Steven drove the truck underneath. He started the engine and climbed into the bin.
The auger, running empty, clattered and shook angrily.
Steven hurried to silence it with quick shovelfuls of barley. He got into a rhythm and was soon lost in the dust
and heat and noise.

When he walked into the house, his father was sitting at the table, turning the dial on Steven's transistor
radio. He had taken it out of the truck while Steven was
inside shovelling. There was another chair at the table and
Steven went over and sat down in it.

His father looked up for a moment, then turned
back to the radio. "I'll take the grain in to the elevator," he
said. "I should be back before dark."

"Leave me the radio," said Steven, still breathing
heavily.

"I'll need it in the truck."

"It's my radio." He could feel the blood rising in his
chest. "I bought it with my own money."

"You can use the one in the pickup," said his father
flatly.

Steven swallowed, tried to speak, but no words came.

———

He lay on his back, hands cupped behind his head, staring up into the darkness. He wanted to turn on his side,
but the smell of grease and sweat from the old mattress
was too strong. His father should have been back hours

ago, but that was nothing new. He might not be back until morning now.

He closed his eyes, and thought he might be falling asleep when the far away sound of a train reached into the silence. The low, steady rumbling of the distant engines was just loud enough to drown out the ringing in his ears. He opened his eyes and saw that the room had become dimly lit by the light from the train. It wasn't long before the noise became too loud to be soothing. He could feel the floor trembling slightly through the mattress.

He remembered some old tracks behind the house, half hidden by tall grass and weeds, but he was sure they hadn't been used for years. He sat up, wide awake.

The room brightened until the featureless walls glowed with strange shapes and shadows. The rumbling became a clattering roar. He tried to sing over it: *"From a jack to a kingggg – from loneliness to a wedding-ringggg."*

The inside of the farmhouse seemed to be on fire. The walls shook violently and tiny dust particles danced crazily in the eerie light. He waited for the train to come crashing into the room.

Then he was at the window, the brightly lit cars of a passenger train screaming past him. A steady stream of lights rushed by, broken only by the split second of darkness between one car and the next.

The train slowed gradually, until the stream of lights separated into individual windows. But there were no faces in any of the windows, looking back out at him. The cars were all empty.

The last car rolled by and there, in the last window,

was the girl he had met that afternoon. She was wearing the same blue dress, holding the cat in her arms—as if she had not put it down since their meeting. She was smiling in that same incredible way, and waving to him.

He waved wildly and shouted for her to wait, then ran out of the house and onto the tracks. She was outside now, standing on the platform at the back of the car. He ran along behind the train, his bare feet slapping harshly against the oily railroad ties. Slowly, slowly, he shortened the distance between himself and the train.

The girl—cat in one arm—leaned over the railing, her free hand reaching out to Steven. The tips of their fingers touched, but in the same instant, the cat squirmed free and jumped. It landed on the tracks in front of Steven and became entangled in his legs.

He fell, scattering the stones between the ties, and lay there, listening to the train clicking away. He lifted his head in time to see two red lights dissolving into the darkness.

———

Steven's father returned to the silent darkness of the farmhouse to find his son sleeping soundly. He lay on the other mattress at the far end of the room, waiting for sleep to come, listening to his son's rhythmic, even breathing.

Then he became aware of something else—something completely unexpected. It sounded like the purring of a cat.

Not Even the Moon

Moonshadows from the tallest pines reached across the deserted road and slipped silently under the wheels of Steven's bicycle. It was all so quiet. A few miles back he had stopped long enough to discover a night so noiseless that the whip of wings from an unseen bird had startled him.

In Haskenfeld there had always been a friendly yard light in view, or a dog barking greetings from a lit porch.

But here, neighbouring farms were concealed from each other by thick woods, and dogs barked with a kind of desperation against all the wildness that waited for them in the primitive darkness. You didn't notice it so much when you were in the car, hiding behind steel and bright lights, but the car was sitting in the yard, next to the house, just as it had been all day.

He had worked right up until sunset before asking, but his father had only said, "You act as if you've got a right to that car. You drive the tractor back and forth across the field a few times, and then you expect to hop in the car and go see your girlfriend."

Don't say anything, he had told himself, it will only be turned against you. And don't let him see your anger. That will finish you for sure.

"Don't give me that look, dammit! Your mother's not here to blubber over you, so forget it. You're not going anywhere."

After that there had only been the same rigid stare from across the table, Steven trying not to look, then giving in only to find the eyes still there, staring him out of existence.

He had thought it might be different, now that it was just the two of them, thought maybe his father would soften a little. But instead, he was worse than ever.

When they'd first arrived, it'd seemed as if things were going to be better. His father had been friendly with the neighbouring farmers that came around. He had even been enthusiastic about the land, which, in truth, was little more than rocks and sand. Once, he had even said,

"It's the best thing we ever did, coming out here."

But after a few months, the same moodiness had come over him again. There had never been any pleasing him, but now he was worse than ever. He spoke only to scold or provoke or humiliate. The other farmers had stopped coming around and things had grown steadily worse, until—it would be two weeks tomorrow—his mother and Trudy had packed some things and left for the city.

Steven would have gone with them, if it wasn't for Marie. She was the only one that mattered now, and he would find a way to see her tonight—even if it was only for a few minutes.

He would surprise her at the diner. Having the car would have meant that she'd sit right next to him, legs tucked up on the seat, her arm on his shoulder, while they drove through town. But as it was, he'd have to walk her home.

The main thing was to get to the diner before it closed. He would ride to the highway on his bike and hitch a ride into town from there. If he made good time and had some luck, he could just make it.

He was coming up on Mazur's Ridge. Somebody had told him it was an old shoreline from a lake that had been there thousands of years ago. It wasn't much compared to the Pembina Hills, but he was up high enough to make out a few of the lights from town. They seemed so far away tonight.

He accelerated down the slope, gliding swiftly over the moonshadows. It felt good to be covering a lot of ground. When the road levelled off again, he pedalled hard to

David H. Elias

keep up his speed, the air cool against his damp shirt.

He looked up at the face of the full moon. It made him feel naked somehow, and fragile, but he couldn't help himself.

"Moonlight poured like milk out of a sable sky," he said out loud. That was a good one. He'd write it down later, and hide it with the others. A few weeks back his father had confronted him with a handful of papers—things he'd written and left on the table in his room.

"You know what this is?" his father had said, closing his fist over the words. "This is shit. Just shit, you hear?" He'd have to be more careful from now on.

New shadows flickered up in the trees and signalled a car coming up behind him. He heard the steady hum of gravel, punctuated by an occasional stone clanking against metal. He slowed down a little and steered the bicycle over to the side of the road.

Maybe it was his father. Maybe, after sitting at the table for a long time, he'd changed his mind about letting him have the car. Maybe he'd changed his mind about everything, and he was coming down the road to say that things would be different from now on.

The car rushed by, the high-speed dust thin in the moonlight, but thick in his throat. He got up off the seat and pedalled hard to make up for lost time.

"When you're in love, time ticks away little pieces of your heart," he spoke. The stuff was just pouring out tonight.

The rolled-up sleeves of his white shirt shone in the moonlight. It was the only clean shirt he'd been able to find. He'd have to start doing some laundry soon.

A small point of light flashed across the road far ahead. That meant it was only about another mile or so to the highway. He caught another slice of light. There were bound to be lots of people on the highway this time of night, heading back into town. He should be able to hitch a ride without too much trouble. It wasn't long before he heard the traffic whining along the asphalt. It gave him extra energy, hearing that, and he pedalled hard until he felt the sweat running down the inside of his shirt.

When he got to the corner, he walked the bike down into the ditch and tried to push it into the opening of the culvert, but the bike was a little too big to fit, so he laid it down in some tall grass and left it there. That would have been a nice touch, for it to slip inside and stay there, ready to go when he came back. But things never seemed to work out that way.

He crossed the highway and set off at a firm pace. When the first car came up behind him he turned around in plenty of time and stuck out his thumb. It wasn't like he hadn't hitchhiked before. Only last week, he'd made it all the way to his uncle's place in Winnipeg, to see Trudy and his mother.

"You know what's funny?" Trudy had said. "I miss him."

"I'm sure he misses you too," Steven had lied.

"Is he going to get better?"

"I don't know."

"Do you think Ma will go back?"

When Steven didn't answer, she went on, "She cries a lot. . . . I hear her talking to Uncle Dick. She keeps saying it's her fault. Uncle Dick says that's baloney.

"Sometimes he gets drunk and calls Pa names. I didn't like when he does that...He took us out for ice cream yesterday.............I had strawberry.....Are you going to stay here?"

"I don't think so."

Two cars came up fast, one right behind the other. Steven had a good feeling about them. The first one honked its horn and kept going, but the second car slowed down. He ran to catch it, but instead of stopping a man leaned out of the window and yelled something he couldn't make out. Then it sped away.

Another car went by without stopping, then another. He was ready to run back for the bike and just ride all the way into town when a car honked its horn and pulled over onto the shoulder. The tail lights flashed a bright red as it came to a stop in front of him. He trotted up to the passenger door and got in.

"Thanks," he said, looking over.

The driver was a black man in a baseball uniform. "Where you headed?" he asked, without looking at Steven.

"Just going into town," Steven answered.

"I'm heading straight through, but I can drop you at the corner."

"Sure, that'd be great."

The driver picked up a pack of cigarettes, put one in his mouth, and held them out to Steven. "You want one?"

"Thanks," said Steven. The driver lit a match and Steven leaned over it. The hand was so steady that he had no trouble. Sometimes it was awkward, doing that.

The black man lit his own cigarette, and said, "Pretty

hard to miss you in the dark with that shirt on." He reached between the seats and pulled out a bottle. He twisted the cap off, took a long swallow, and passed it across.

Steven took hold of the bottle, and as casually as he could, tipped it back and sipped. He swallowed quickly and passed the bottle back.

"You got a girl—in town?" the black man asked before taking another drink.

"That's right," answered Steven, the taste still bitter in his mouth. "How'd you know?"

"What else would you be doing hitchhiking this time of night. The black man took a long drag on his cigarette. "No wheels, eh?" he said.

"No wheels," Steven echoed.

"Fella's gotta have wheels if he wants to keep a girl." He took another pull on the bottle and passed it over. "Girls like to get driven around. Makes 'em feel special."

"I usually have a car," said Steven, "but I had some trouble."

"What kind of trouble?" said the black man.

The corner was approaching. "You can drop me off here," said Steven.

The driver pulled over and Steven opened the door. "Thanks for the ride."

"Sure," said the black man. "That girl," he added, "the one you're going to meet. She must be pretty special."

"She is," answered Steven. "Thanks again."

It was half a mile from the corner into town. When he got to Main Street, he turned east and headed for the diner. He could see the poorly lit metal sign with the words SNACK STOP running vertically along it.

It really wasn't much of a place. Some padded stools along a washed-out counter and a row of small booths down the opposite wall. Everyone in school called it the greasy spoon. Steven wasn't sure what that meant, but it didn't sound very good.

When he looked through the window, he was surprised to see some kids from school sitting at the counter. There wasn't usually anyone his age at the diner. They all hung around at Nick's, on the other end of town. The customers here were mostly men his father's age—the kind that wore work clothes and ate with dirty hands.

Sometimes, while he was waiting for Marie to finish up, he'd make small talk with them—about everyday stuff, maybe a piece of machinery, or the weather. People like that never thought of themselves as superior. He was pleased that they took a liking to him, but Marie never seemed very impressed by any of it.

He recognized Jerry right away. Everyone knew who he was. Marie was standing across from him, on the other side of the counter. She was wiping her hands across the front of her blue uniform, and laughing at something Jerry was saying.

There were two other people with him, a guy and a girl. He knew they were going steady because they walked around the halls at noon together, just the way he and Marie did, but he didn't think she knew them to talk to.

Jerry was pretty dressed up, as usual. Even in school, he always wore clothes that looked really expensive. Tonight he was wearing an amber sports jacket, with grey slacks. Some of the guys made fun of him behind his back, but the girls all thought he was cool.

Marie was always pointing him out at school and saying things like, "You should get a pair of boots like that," or, "You should get your hair cut like that."

Jerry's hair was jet black and straight. Steven's was blond and curly. He had tried slicking it back with lots of hair tonic and water, but it just didn't want to stay that way. As soon as it dried out, the curls would spring away from his head and make him look ridiculous.

He opened the door and Marie looked up to see who it was. The way her expression changed made him feel like an intruder. Back on the road, he had pictured the way her face would break into a smile when he came in through the door of the diner. But the way she looked now wasn't anything like that.

She brightened a little when he stepped up to the counter.

"Hi," she said.

"Hi," he answered.

The others looked up at him, then glanced at each other in a way that made him uncomfortable.

He sat down, leaving an empty stool between himself and the others. Nobody said anything. Marie kept staring at his shirt. He looked down at the white material and saw that it was soaked through with sweat in several places, but worse than that, the wet patches were a dirty grey colour. Maybe it was dust from the road. Or maybe he'd washed in too much of a hurry. Either way, it looked pretty awful.

Jerry got up and the others started for the door.

"Maybe we'll see you later," Jerry said to Marie.

"Sure," said Marie over her shoulder. She was headed for the back of the diner, her hands up behind her neck.

When Steven looked up they were out on the sidewalk, laughing and shaking their heads. Then they all got into Jerry's car and drove off.

Marie came back along the front side of the counter, a purse in one hand and a sweater draped over her arm.

"Look at you. What happened?"

"I don't know."

"What were you doing?"

"Nothing."

"You look like you came straight off the field."

"I'm sorry."

Marie headed for the door. "You didn't say you were coming tonight."

"I know. I just wanted to see you."

When they were out on the sidewalk, she said, "I have to go straight home."

"I'll walk you."

"Where's the car?"

"I didn't bring it."

"How did you get here?"

"I hitchhiked."

"Steven, what's going on?"

"Nothing, I just wanted to come into town and walk you home. What's wrong with that?"

They headed quickly down the sidewalk. "What did they want?" asked Steven.

"Who?"

"You know, Jerry and the others."

"Oh, there's a party over at Eddie's house."

"He invited you?"

"It's not like I'm going or anything."

"But he asked you to go?"

"Let's just forget it, okay?" said Marie.

When they got to the house, Marie stopped at the gate. "I'd better go in," she said.

Steven stepped toward her. He kissed her, but it was only for a second.

"I have to go," she said.

"Couldn't we go somewhere? Just for a few minutes?"

"Maybe if you had the car." She put her hand on the latch of the gate.

"What did Jerry say?"

"What do you mean?"

"Back at the diner. He said something funny."

"What are you talking about?"

"He said something that made you laugh."

"I don't know. I don't remember. What does it matter?"

"I just wondered what he said, that's all."

"I have to go in."

He kissed her again, a little longer this time, but her hand stayed on the gate.

"I'll see you in school," she said, and went through the gate. He waited until the door closed behind her, then turned and started back up the street. He thought of stopping off at Nick's for a plate of fries and gravy, but he didn't want anybody to see him with his shirt like it was.

When he got back out to the highway, the moon was setting in the west. There were no cars in sight. The air was a lot cooler, and he was shivering. He broke into a run to try and work up some heat, but running made him feel out of control somehow, and he slowed quickly back to a walk.

He looked down at his shirt. It glowed a white neon under the moonlight. And the stains didn't show up at all. It looked perfectly clean. Maybe, if he'd met Marie by moonlight, she might never have noticed the stains, and everything would still be all right.

He was halfway to the turnoff when a car finally came up behind him. He could hear the engine working and the tires scrubbing the asphalt. He wanted it to be the black baseball player. He wanted to smoke another cigarette and drink some more from the bottle. He wanted to tell him everything that happened and maybe even make-up a line or two, just to show off. "It was the sweat and dirt on the clean white shirt that caused the hurt," he'd say. He should have turned and put out his thumb, but instead he stood and watched as the car sped past him. Only he could see everything that was going on inside.

The dashboard flooded the interior with a penetrating green light. It turned Jerry's shiny black hair the colour of mica, and dyed his amber jacket a deep brown.

It created sensuous shadows along the calves of Marie's legs, tucked up on the seat—glowed pale against her hand, where it rested on his shoulder, jade fingers spread apart, sliding back and forth over the smooth chestnut material.

The tip of one finger disappeared under the lapel of Jerry's jacket, and when it reappeared, it turned slowly toward the window, until it was pointing at Steven's shirt, at the olive stain there, growing larger even as he stared down at it.

When he raised his head, the car was gone. He took off the shirt while he walked, and let it fall in the road. There was no one to stop him, not even the moon.

Lucky Strike

When the professor of English finally walked into the room, a number of students (one of them scowling at his watch) had already left. Those who had stayed now settled into an uneven layer of muffled noises. The girls picked up their pens and crossed their legs. The boys slid back in their seats.

The professor tossed a paperback onto the desk at

the front and continued on to the far side of the room. The floor sighed under his soft-soled shoes. He pushed against one of the large, dirty windows and swung it wide open. The new air carried a cool blend of musty leaves and mist into the room.

He wore a camel-coloured sports jacket that fit tight across his shoulders, accentuating his stocky build. His blond hair was straight and cut very short. His nose and lips were thick and coarse. He might have been thirty-five, but the lines around his eyes and along his forehead looked deeper than that. In Steven's movie he was a washed-up prizefighter staring out of a cheap hotel window.

The professor reached into the side pocket of his jacket and took out a crumpled pack of cigarettes. Cellophane crackled. He shook the package once, and a single white cylinder appeared. He pulled it out with two fingers, tapped it against the back of his hand, and placed it at the very corner of his mouth. It hung there at a brutal angle. He flattened his large hand and pulled a lighter out of the front pocket of his blue jeans. When he opened it, the lid fell back with a smart, metallic click. The rasp of steel on flint came once, twice, three times, before a pale flame puffed up.

The professor stared at the flame for a moment, then brought it slowly up to the cigarette. Steven was surprised to see a light, but rapid trembling in the professor's hand. Smoke simmered off the glowing tip. The exotic smell of Turkish tobacco filled the room.

He turned, and through a long cloud of blue smoke, looked—for the first time—at the young men and women who sat in silence before him. He clipped the lighter shut. With the same fluttering hand that held the cigarette, and now the lighter as well, he picked a piece of tobacco from the corner of his mouth and rubbed it out of existence between his thumb and middle finger.

He took another pull on the cigarette and said, "I want you to read something." The words came out thick and smooth, and smoke poured out between them. He walked to the desk and picked up the paperback. "This book. *The Sun Also Rises* by Ernest Hemingway. We'll talk about it next week." And he walked out of the room.

The girls uncrossed their legs and began to chatter immediately amongst themselves, in a way that allowed Steven, who was listening, to understand exactly nothing. The boys picked up their notebooks and left.

Steven waited until after five, but when he got to the bookstore there were still long lineups. He found the novel quickly and got in behind an engineer who was holding onto the biggest, thickest textbook Steven had ever seen. When the engineer got to the front of the line he brought the book down on the counter with an intimidating thud. The cashier gave him a look. He grinned back, took a lot of money out of his wallet, and paid for the thing. Then he picked it up with both hands and walked off, carrying the book like a block of cement. When Steven placed his copy of *The Sun Also Rises* on the counter, it made almost no sound at all.

That night, just before going to sleep, he decided to read a few pages. He really wasn't much of a reader. The novels they'd read in high school—*Return of the Native,*

David H. Elias

Pride and Prejudice—had been tough to get through. He got into bed and lit a cigarette. He picked up the book, cracked the binding, and began to read.

————

When he turned the last page, daylight was seeping in through the small window, absorbing the lamp light. He had never read a book in one sitting before. He felt as if a year had passed.

He closed the book, looked at the cover, and placed it on the table beside the bed. He stirred around in the loaded ashtray to make sure he hadn't left a cigarette burning. Then he turned off the lamp and fell asleep.

At the beginning of the next class, the professor repeated the same ritual, even down to the tiny particle of tobacco—real or imagined—that he removed, with a quivering hand, from the corner of his mouth.

"What do you think was wrong with Jake?" he asked through the smoke. "Anyone?"

The professor seemed to be staring directly at him. He raised his hand.

"You don't have to do that here," the professor said flatly. "You're not in high school anymore."

Steven brought his hand down quickly.

"Well?" said the professor.

"He was im*po*tent," said Steven, pronouncing the word with the accent on the second syllable.

"The word is *im*potent," corrected the professor. Ste-

116

ven felt a hot ringing in his ears. It was like Chi-Who
A-Who-A all over again. That had been in grade ten. He
had been reading aloud from a story about Mexico. He
remembered the sentence: "The little Chihuahua barked
and snapped at the horse's heels." He had never seen the
word before. He pronounced it "Chi-Who-A-Who-A." The
other kids had laughed until he wanted to run out of the
school and never come back.

Months later, someone would come up to him and
say "Chi-Who-A-Who-A!" and stagger off laughing. Once a
plowboy, always a plowboy.

"Young lady." The professor walked up to a girl in
the front row and stood over her. Steven was thankful
he'd turned his attention to someone else. "Do you know
what that means?" The girl had long, auburn hair that was
wavy and thick, not straight like most of the girls. Steven
had noticed her the first day. She was wearing the same
tiny black leather vest. Her good looks both attracted and
intimidated him. That was nothing new.

"It means he can't perform," she offered, her voice
tentative.

"Can't perform what?"

"He can't be her lover."

"Whose lover?"

"Brett? Is that her name?"

"But he is in love with her, isn't he?"

"Yes, but he can't make love with her."

"Why not?"

"Because he's—what he said." She turned her head
and pointed a finger at the back of the room. "He's impotent."

"But what does that mean exactly?"

No one said anything.

"Let's spell it out."

Steven could see she was very uncomfortable.

"It means, ladies and gentlemen—" and he took a long pull on his cigarette— "that he can't copulate with her because he got his penis shot off in the war." When he said "penis" a lot of smoke poured out. Someone coughed. The redhead blushed deeply. She looked vulnerable just then, with the blood rushing up to her face. Steven thought he might be in love.

In his movie they would bump into each other after class and talk about how embarrassed they had both been. Then they would just laugh about it and walk down the hall together, away from the camera.

When class was over, he followed her out of the room. Her mini-skirt was wrinkled at the back where she had sat on it. The wrinkles made her skirt even shorter, but not in an attractive kind of way. He wanted to reach out and give it a firm tug. I wonder, he thought, if girls know what they look like from the back with those things on. He wanted to catch up to her and say something, but he had never been able to do that kind of thing, at least not sober.

He didn't know how to approach women, never had. He thought of Marie, and missed her suddenly. Things would be so different if she were here. He wished more women were like her.

One day Marie had just come right up to him and asked him if he wanted to go out with her. One minute she had been standing across the hall from him, and the next she was asking him if he wanted to go to a movie. She had stood there, waiting for an answer, her eyes on his. He had thought it was very brave of her, and decided not only to go out to the movies, but to fall in love with her then and there.

All through the movie he had sat with his arm around her warm shoulders. Out of the corner of his eye he could see her blouse rising and falling, and her head turning to look at him once in awhile. A few times, she had moved herself up against him.

Later, at her front door, he had kissed her. Her hands had come up quickly to grasp his shoulders, her lips pressing hard on his. Then she had brought her face back, her eyes searching his. "Why didn't you do that sooner?" she had asked in a tight voice.

"I didn't know if you wanted me to."

She had looked at him then, in that way—the way that others sometimes did. The way that Brett Ashley must have looked at Jake Barnes.

Once, after they had been dating for some time, she had revealed to him all the little things she had done to get his attention.

"You remember that time in the hall, when I smiled at you?" she said. "Didn't you notice me smiling at you?"

"Well sure but ... "

"Or the time I got in line behind you in the gymnasium. And I said those things?"

"Actually I ... "

"I was embarrassed about it afterward. Especially when you didn't even ask me out."

"I would have ... if ...."

"And what about that time I sat with Paul in Vicki's. And then you came in, and I moved over to your side?"

"But how was I supposed to know what that meant? I just thought you were being friendly."

"Being friendly? I ... Oh, never mind." There was that look again. "How can anyone so smart be so stupid?"

As the semester wore on, there were fewer and fewer empty seats in the English professor's class. The front row became a chorus line of giggling girls with tiny skirts and big eyes. Their heavy perfumes collaborated to overpower the breeze that came in through the big open window. When they crossed their legs, they pressed their thighs together so lustily that even he, Steven, could pick up the signals they were sending.

"What do the two rose petals symbolize in that passage?" the professor would ask about a poem they had been studying. One of the girls in the front row—without raising her hand—would say, "Maybe they symbolize lips— his lover's lips?"

"But what kind of lips?"

The confused girl would wriggle in her seat. "Her lips, you know, her mouth."

"His lover's mouth?" the professor would tease.

"Yes, that's it."

"No, no, no!" he would scold. "That's not it. The two rose petals"—a long pull on his cigarette—"symbolize the two red and swollen lips of her mons veneris!" The girl in the little black vest would blush, while the professor crushed the cigarette under his shoe.

One day after class, just as Steven was leaving, the professor called him up to the front. "I wanted to see you," he said, "about that essay of yours. Talk to you about some of your ideas."

"Sure."

"But not here. Listen, I'm having some students over to the house this Saturday. Why don't you come, and we'll talk about it then?"

"Okay, I guess so."

"Fine."

"See you then." Steven headed quickly for the door.

"Just a minute. Don't you want the address?"

"Oh, yeah, right."

The professor tore up an empty pack of Lucky Strikes and wrote the address on the inside. When Steven took it out of his trembling hand the professor held onto it for a little while and looked right at him.

"Come anytime."

Steven wanted to get out of the room as quickly as possible. It was always like that with this kind of thing. It was important to get away when people you were uncomfortable with were being nice. Get out and end the scene.

———

When Steven got to the house, he walked back out to a street lamp and checked the address again. It didn't seem like the right place—an old three-story house in a run-down neighbourhood. If it had not been for cracks of light at some of the windows he might have turned around and gone home. He had imagined a stately old home with a big porch, or maybe a bungalow with a pool, but this?

He walked around the back and rang the doorbell several times. There was no answer. He tried knocking but that didn't bring any response either. He could hear voices and the muffled sound of music. Finally he just opened the door and peeked in. There were a lot of people. A few of them looked over his way, then turned back to their conversations.

He stepped inside and shoved the case of beer he had brought onto the nearest counter. He took one out and drank it on the spot. The case was already half empty. He had been priming for some time. Priming was something he always did when he was going into a strange situation. This situation felt stranger than most, so there had been a lot of priming to do. Still, he felt far too sober.

He opened another bottle and looked around. The inside of the house looked just as bad as the outside. Even in the dim candlelight he could see that the paint on the kitchen walls was cracked and peeling. The floor was filthy, and the stove was practically out of sight.

In the next room, the furniture consisted of a wicker chair, a waterbed, and a stereo perched on some uneven brick and wood shelving. Candles and incense burned here and there around the room. A black and white poster of Janis Joplin covered one of the windows. She had the microphone in her mouth, her face and body contorted and sweating, her hair chaos. Her shirt was torn open and the top button of her blue jeans was undone.

"She's one of the few women to make it big without looks." It was the professor.

"Oh, good evening, sir," said Steven, turning.

The professor was wearing the same camel-coloured jacket and blue jeans that he wore in class. He was looking up at the poster, studying it intently. He brought a bottle of wine up to his lips and took several noisy swallows.

"Lots of women become famous," the professor continued, still staring, "even though they have little or no talent." He turned to Steven. "What they do have is a sweet face and a great set of tits."

Some one with long brown hair and square glasses passed the professor a roll-your-own cigarette. Steven recognized it instantly as a joint. The professor took a long pull on it, inhaled deeply, and passed it on to Steven, who did the same as if it were nothing new for him.

He held his breath and watched the professor out of the corner of his eye, exhaling only after he did. "She was one of a kind, all right," said the professor, his voice hoarse from the smoke. "She refused to make herself glamorous. That way, people had to deal with her talent."

He took another swig from the bottle. "On the other hand, men will always be suckers for a good pair of tits."

It was like that for the rest of the evening. Steven followed the professor in and out of circles, smoking dope, and listening to him say outrageous things. He found himself mumbling things like, "Right on, man" and "Far out."

At one point the professor put his arm around Steven while he was talking. Then he stood up right in the middle of the room and shouted, "For God's sake hold your tongue and let me love!" It was a line from one of the poems they had been studying. Steven had no idea what it meant.

He followed the professor, who was staggering a little, up the stairs, and in the doorway of a room, the professor's face invaded his. Then his whole body came up against Steven's and the wine bottle pushed up between his legs. Steven pulled himself free and hurried away.

———

It was late. John Lennon was chanting, "Number nine, number nine, number nine." There weren't as many people now. Steven took a joint from the girl next to him and saw that it was the redhead. Instead of her little black vest, she was wearing a little red vest, and she was barefoot. Her toenails were a bright, shiny red.

"Can I ask you a personal question?" said Steven. He didn't wait for a reply. "I was just wondering, when you're wearing your little black vest, are your toenails black, too?"

"What?" She probably didn't recognize him, but then why should she? Ever since the second coming of Chi-Who-A-Who-A, he hadn't said a word in class.

"Nothing," he said. "Never mind."

She looked away. Then she looked back and said,

"You're stoned."

"What if I am?"

"You have the silliest grin on your face."

Steven grinned even wider.

"You look like the cat that ate the canary."

"You mean like Sylvester Pussycat." He spat the words out in a cartoon voice.

"You're really stoned."

"Right, and you're not."

"Not stoned enough." She reached over. "Pass that back. I want some more."

He let her take it.

"I didn't see you before."

"I was upstairs with my boyfriend. He's passed out up there. Him and the professor both."

"That's too bad."

"No, it's all right. He wouldn't like me doing this anyway."

"Doing what?"

"You know, grass."

Steven looked up at the poster of Janis Joplin. "Do you think it's important to have a nice pair of tits?" he asked.

"I could slap your face."

"Sorry. I'm sorry."

"You're not the professor, you know."

There was a long silence. "I saw what happened," she said.

"What happened where?"

"With the professor. Up there." She pointed up the

stairs. "It's all right." She put a hand on his shoulder. "He made a pass at me too."

They smoked some more.

"Did you let him?" asked Steven.

There was a long pause before she said, "No," and then added, "Did you?"

He turned to look at her. She was grinning wildly.

"No," he smiled.

Once they started laughing, they couldn't seem to stop.

The Last Visitor

———

JAW MOVES UP   DOWN   UP DOWN
SQUARE JAW SQUARE
SOLID
DARK MOUTH
TONGUE FLASHES   PINK   DARTING TONGUE

LIPS THINNING   THICKENING

                                    CURLING

                    PINK EARTHWORM LIPS

SQUIRMING

                         HEADS TAILS PINCHED

          FLAT WHITE TEETH

                              TEETH of the FATHER

What are the WORDS?

What are the words from the LIPS of the FATHER?

The FATHER to the SON?

WORDS?

Unrecognizable POCKETS of NOISE

Transparent POUCHES of liquid GARBLE

WOBBLING through the vacant air.

SPLASHING against the bare walls.

WORDS are not the source of POWER.

EYES have the POWER.

EYES of the FATHER.

POWER to make the son crawl deep inside himself.
To make him search the DARKEST corners of his soul.

To try and discover what is hidden there, that the EYES of
the father see, but the EYES of the son do not.

The eyes of the father are BURNING lakes of fire, fed by
HOT rivers of angry concentration. Their heat pushes you away
—pins you back against yourself.

Who could withstand their ferocity for even a second?
Who could endure long enough to search there—for the softness
that a
     son's

         heart

             needs.

"What are you staring at?" When Steven didn't answer, his father got up off the chair and stood in the middle of the room.

"Look at this place ... no wonder you're depressed. Couldn't they put some pictures on the wall? Not even curtains ... what harm could it do to have curtains?"

His father lifted a heavy pair of glasses away from his eyes FIERCE and held them there. With his other hand he rubbed the bridge of his nose, then lowered the glasses back into place.

He turned to look down at Steven. "If you're just going to sit there, I'm leaving. I didn't come all this way just to watch you sit on that bed and stare into space."

He started for the door. "If it was up to me, they never would have put you in here ... you can't trust these people, none of them."

He pulled the big door back, then stopped. A small, man in a Hawaiian shirt stood in the doorway.

It was Peter. He took a quick step forward, brought his right arm up and held it out, the way someone would if he were checking his watch. But of course, he wasn't wearing a watch. That wasn't allowed.

He pointed to a spot just above the wrist bone. "You see that?" he said, his eyes fixed on those of Steven's father. "That hair there?" The words echoed loudly into the room. "There." He kept bringing the arm closer, until Steven's father had to take a step back.

"That hair there? It's not mine."

Steven got up from the bed, walked to the door, and leaned around his father's shoulder. Peter turned to look at him. "Not mine," he pleaded, shaking his head.

Steven nodded. That was all you had to do. Just nod. Peter lowered his arm and moved away down the hall.

Steven slipped past his father and headed in the direction of the lounge. When he walked by the long white desk, the nurse smiled up at him. It was a stupid smile—the kind that people wear when they don't care whether you smile back or not.

He ignored it, continued on to the lounge and took his place in the soft chair next to the window. The others were in their usual spots: the Native woman on the big wooden chair against the far wall, rocking back and forth in quick, stiff strokes, holding the same dirty rag over her face. The Bible man, squatting on stick legs over a book on the floor, reciting the same verse over and over—one long finger tracing across the page, worn through where the words used to be.

The Native woman would soon lift the wrinkled cloth away from her face to reveal two flat, dark holes where her nose ought to be. Her eyes would widen, head tilted back, before she opened her toothless mouth to fling one quick convulsion of laughter across the room. Then the rag would come back over her face.

The Bible man would lift his thin, greasy face to scowl at her before turning back to his scripture.

Steven's father had followed him as far as the desk. He was resting his hands on the edge of the counter, saying something to the nurse with the phoney smile. After a minute, she came out from behind the counter, took a key out of her pocket, and unlocked the elevator.

The bell rang, and when the doors opened with a low rumble, his father, without so much as a sideways glance, disappeared between them.

Another father would have kept walking, straight ahead, past the desk, past the nurse with the phoney smile. He would have come right into the lounge and sat down on the sofa next to the window. But that would have been somebody else's father.

Steven leaned over the side of the chair and looked out of the window at the people on the street, far below. Looking down like that, about all you could see were their shoulders and the tops of their heads. When they walked, their shoes slid back and forth underneath them like a puppet's. Two girls in bright yellow jackets caught his attention. He thought one of them might be pretty, but it was hard to tell from up here.

After a few minutes the top of his father's head appeared. He imagined it tilting up to look at him. It might be all right that way. But his father did not look up. Nobody ever did.

The bell rang and the elevator doors opened again. A thin girl in a white smock stepped out between two policemen. They led her over to the desk and started talking to the nurse with the phoney smile. He saw that she had been badly beaten.

She stood between them, head down, staring at her bare feet. He was just thinking that she might be pretty if she didn't have those two black eyes when—without raising her head—she turned to look at him, her eyes locked on his.

By the time he managed to tear himself away, he could only catch his breath in short, shallow gulps. He ran past her, into his room, slamming the door behind him.

———

Trudy didn't mind the lounge so they sat on one of the soft couches, drinking coffee from styrofoam cups.

She reached down to pull up her pant leg. "Look at this." For a second Steven thought it might be a miracle, but then he saw that the leg was as thin and withered as ever.

"Notice anything different?"

He hadn't really taken much notice of her leg for a long time, but it didn't seem any different.

"No brace! Isn't that great? Doctor Loewen says I might never have to wear one again—as long as I keep up my physio."

She let the pant leg fall back over her shin and straightened up. She picked up the coffee cup, took a sip, then held the edge of the cup between her lips for a moment before she pulled it away.

"He said something else." She looked into the cup. "He said I'm the last person in Manitoba to get polio. Can you believe that? Nobody ever gets it anymore." She looked up at Steven. "I wish he hadn't told me that. It's a funny thing to tell someone, don't you think?"

A wild cackle spilled from the far end of the room. Steven ignored it.

"Remember how you used to take me for walks be-

cause the doctor said it was good for my leg? Remember
what you used to do? You'd walk faster and faster until I
couldn't keep up anymore. I'd fall behind and call after
you, but you'd just keep going like you didn't hear me.

"I'd start crying and then you'd stop, turn around,
and hold your arms out to me. I'd run as fast as I could
and when I'd caught up to you, you'd pick me up and
give me a big hug. You used to do that every time."

For the first time since he'd arrived in this place,
Steven wanted to say something, but he just couldn't
think of any words.

"I never told you this before," Trudy went on, "but,
after the first few times, I wasn't really scared anymore. I
knew you wouldn't leave me. I cried anyway."

Peter shuffled down the hall and stopped at the long
white desk. He hung one arm over the counter and
shouted at the nurse, "Not mine." She smiled in exactly
the same way that she always did.

"I don't mind it that you don't talk to me, but you
should talk to the doctor. She won't let you out of here
unless you do. You know that, don't you? You have to tell
her something."

The Native woman rocked back and forth in her
chair, the cloth over her face.

"It's funny. I always thought I'd end up here first,"
said Trudy.

Steven leaned against the window sill and looked
down at the street. The Bible man spat scripture at the
floor, the words fast and frantic. The chaotic babbling
sounded to Steven like someone talking in his sleep.

"Do you think it would've been any different if we'd grown up in an Italian family? You remember Francesca, don't you? You met her at Grampa's funeral. He would've like her."

"Anyway, she's Italian. I go over to their house a lot. At first I couldn't stand it, but now I'm always over there. It's pretty wild, especially at the supper table. There's always wine and everybody talks at once. And they're always touching each other—hugging and kissing.

"The first few times it really threw me, just to be someplace where people do that all the time. But now, whenever I go over there, I always get at least one hug."

The bell rang and the elevator doors opened. Nobody came out. They closed again.

"Remember that time we went to the zoo? That was my first trip to the city. I wanted to see all the big buildings and the streets and the traffic and the people. But all we did was go to the zoo.

"We spent all afternoon watching the hyena. Remember? I go back there now, sometimes, just to see him. He's still there, you know, still pacing back and forth on that stupid platform of his.

"We could go on Sunday—if you like. The doctor said it would be all right to go for an hour or two. We don't have to go to the zoo if you don't want to. We could go someplace else. Maybe someplace in the country.

"I don't like the city. I never did, really, except for the first five minutes." Trudy looked down at the brown paper bag in her lap. She had worked her hands back and forth along the folded top until it was wrinkled and shiny.

"I brought you some more clothes." She held the bag by its smooth sides and placed it on the table in front of her.

Steven looked down at the bag, then across at his sister. Sunday school songs twirled around inside his head as he watched her blink out a tear, then rub it away before it could run down the side of her nose.

———

Steven lay on the bed, staring up at the ceiling. The naked light bulb hurt his eyes, but he held them there as long as he could. When he couldn't stand it any longer, he closed them and tried to sleep, but it was no use. The medication wasn't kicking in tonight. He sat up at the end of the bed and looked out into the hallway.

He stared for a long time, but no one appeared. There was always someone—a nurse with a tray, an orderly with a cart—but not tonight. And the night sounds—a phone ringing, a shoe squeaking, the elevator bell—weren't there either.

And then he heard the slap of bare feet echoing down the corridor. She was coming for him. The shadow of a figure slid across the threshold, darkening the smooth, hard floor. His heart beat in hard, heavy pumps, each one deeper than the one before, each one filling the chambers to bursting, then emptying them with an enormous contraction that sent a tremor rumbling through his chest.

A thin white ankle appeared.

A shock of blood pulsed through his neck and

into his skull, throwing his head back against the wall. His hands throbbed. Blood rushed into his fingertips, threatening to burst through the skin and shoot across the bed. The girl with the two black eyes stopped in the doorway, and turned to look into the room.

It started with a simple, modest thinning of the lips—a small curling at the corners of the mouth—then it widened until the lips parted, revealing sharp, white teeth—stretched to reveal the gums, red and lumpy—continued to grow until the mouth seemed about to tear itself apart.

The air became elastic—he couldn't get his lungs around it, only stretch it a short way down his throat before it snapped back out. The girl with the two black eyes waited in the doorway, her face a grotesque, grinning mask. With the last bit of air he could capture, Steven carved out the only two words he could think of.

"Come in," he said.

Dust Devils

———

Cold sunlight streamed in through the broken window of the farmhouse. It fell on Steven as he slept—curled up under blankets and clothes on the soiled, damp mattress. His eyes fluttered and he squinted into the light. The first thing he saw was a bare wall, and for just a second he thought he was back in the lockup.

He threw back the covers and sat up. His breath

came out in white clouds visible only within the sharp
boundaries formed by the shaft of light. The sunlight was
bright, but at this time of morning it carried no heat. As
the day progressed the house would warm rapidly, but he
would be gone long before then.

He dressed quickly and walked over to the table and
chairs that made up the only furniture in the house. He lit
the Coleman stove and placed a pot of water on one ele-
ment and a frying pan on the other. The grease at the
bottom of the frying pan turned from white to transparent
and began to bubble. The water hissed softly as it heated.
The cooking sounds were comforting.

If his mother were still at home, she would be working in the kitchen by now. She might be singing softly to
herself, the way she sometimes did when things were
quiet. "If Teardrops were Pennies and Heartaches were
Gold" or maybe "Mansion on the Hill."

He ate his meal in silence, enjoying the taste of the
eggs and the warmth of the coffee and Carnation milk. He
was longing for warmth now, but in a few hours he
would be cursing the heat. He drank a second cup of
coffee and thought about Saturday. That was the day his
father was coming back for him. The last thing he'd said
before leaving was, "I expect that field to be done when I get
back. There's no substitute for hard work. It's the best thing
for you now. Besides, you need some time to yourself."

When he stepped out into the farmyard, the first thing
he did was look at the sky. This morning it was blue from
horizon to horizon—perfect, clean and pure. You could look
up at a sky like that and feel your whole life beginning

again, as if you had been reborn into a new world.

But even as Steven let that vast, blue space absorb him, he knew the vision wouldn't last. In a few hours he would look to the west and see clouds gathering on the horizon. With their flat bottoms and fluffy white tops, they would come sailing across the sky. Their motion would be just slow enough to pass unnoticed, but sooner than you would ever think possible, they would be over-head, their shadows moving over the flat countryside with remarkable speed.

And he would welcome them. They would provide him with intermittent shade as he made his way back and forth across the huge field. They would bring a breeze to keep the exhaust of the motor from suffocating him, a breeze that would cool his dry, dust-covered skin.

He walked briskly across the farmyard, past the empty outbuildings, and through some long grass toward the tractor sitting at the edge of the field. Nothing seemed to be stirring this morning. Finally he spotted one lone gopher, popping its head up and down, front paws tucked neatly under its chin, eyes bulging with tension and life. He stepped up onto the steel tracks of the Cater-pillar tractor and placed his lunch on the seat. He grabbed the crank, walked along the tracks to the front, and jumped down. He locked the crank into position, then stood motionless, searching every part of his body for strength. He tightened his grip on the crank and then, using all of his body weight, forced it down. When his feet touched the ground, he swung to the left and pushed up with his legs and back. That was half a turn. You could compress two cylinders that way, and if one of them fired, there was a good chance a few more would fire after it.

His father could grab the crank and spin it completely around, never stopping until the engine ran smoothly. He imagined what it would be like to have that much strength. Someday he would manage it.

By the time he got the engine running on its own he had generated enough heat to send the chill out of his body. He sat back in the cushioned seat of the tractor. It wasn't the most comfortable seat, with some of the springs collapsed and part of the upholstery torn away, but it felt just fine this morning.

He took out his tobacco and papers. For years he had watched his grandfather roll and light his cigarettes—had noticed how much comfort he took from that simple act. The world would stop for a little while. The mindless, back-breaking labour would wait a few minutes while the sweet smell of freshly lit tobacco filled the air.

One day, without a word, his grandfather had casually held the tobacco out to him. And so he had taken it and rolled a crooked, uneven cigarette—had cupped his hands around those of his grandfather's to light it. And then, under the shade of the granary, they had smoked together, making small talk about the day's work and the weather. Ever since then it had been a special ritual for him.

To test whether the engine was warm enough, Steven walked along the steel tracks and bent down beside the muffler. In spite of the noise, fumes and heat, he held the end of the cigarette against the base of the muffler. With a few good pulls he managed to light it. The engine was ready.

He straightened up and turned to scan the horizon. No clouds yet, but it was still early. It certainly was a quiet morning. From endless hours of looking out across the flat, even prairie, he had developed a keen eye for the tiniest movement or detail.

But now, as he swept his eyes over the countryside, he felt that the rest of the world must still be asleep, and that the loud rumbling of the tractor was an intrusion on its slumber.

Most of the places around were abandoned, like this one. The farmers who once lived on them had given up and sold out to big operators like his father. The ones who were left kept their distance. He thought of something his grandfather had once said: "Would a dying man welcome a vulture?"

He sat down on the cushion and pushed the throttle lever as far forward as it would go. The engine died momentarily, as the fuel mixture changed from gasoline to diesel. Then new and powerful vibrations shook the tractor. Hard concussions sounded deep inside the engine and black smoke billowed up out of the muffler.

He manoeuvred the tractor over the weed-covered earth towards the cultivator, far out in the field. As he travelled, he gauged how much of the field still had to be worked. It might be possible to finish by Saturday.

David H. Elias

The sun was directly overhead when he decided to stop for lunch. No clouds had come rolling out of the west to shade him from the intense heat—no breeze to carry away the dust kicked up by the steel tracks. Instead, the dust had settled on his bare shoulders and arms, while the exhaust fumes carried straight back from the muffler into his face, choking him.

His ears rang. The steel tracks were always loud, but today they sounded like a thousand clanging bells pounding noise into his ears. Tonight, when he lay exhausted, aching for sleep, the ringing would keep him awake. Each night it grew louder and stayed longer.

He didn't want to stop, but he knew he should get out of the sun for a while. At the end of the field, where a few small shrubs grew, he jumped off the tractor. Sitting in the sparse shade, he drank long and deep from a quart jar filled with cold coffee.

Even the long stems of grass stood motionless, the way they would in the dead of a still summer night. The noise of countless insects filled the warm, thick air.

There was something out in the field. He watched in fascination as a tiny, swirling funnel of dust moved across the field. He'd seen them before. They formed only on hot days when the air was perfectly still. They were like miniature tornadoes. He spotted another one. The funnel on this one writhed and curled, then disappeared as it crossed the edge of the field.

He scanned the field carefully to see if he could
watch one starting up. But they always seemed to come
from an area he had not been watching. They didn't look
big enough to do any real harm. Still, their erratic movement, and the menacing curl of their funnels, had a
disturbing effect.

When he had finished his meal he felt sleepy. A nap
in the shade would be welcome. He could avoid the worst
heat of the day and wake up refreshed, ready for a full
afternoon and evening of work. But valuable time would
be lost. He climbed back onto the shaking tractor and
throttled up.

By mid-afternoon the senseless din of the machinery ham-
mered against the boy's skull. The relentless heat, mixed
with the dust, crackled and prickled his skin. He wanted
a cigarette, but he found that his lungs could not manage
the dust and smoke at the same time. The tractor under
his feet was so hot that he had to lean back on the seat
and let his boots rest on the canopy.

Dust devils swirled behind and in front of him. It
had taken him a long time, but he had finally managed to
discover the pattern they followed. They always started at
the border where the freshly turned soil lay, then moved
off toward the edge of the field and died.

After that he had become drowsy, until the noise of
the tractor seemed to be coming from a distance, and

then he was moving forward in silence, as if he were part of a movie in which the sound had suddenly been turned off. The edge of the field wasn't getting any nearer. The tractor seemed to be suspended just above the ground, not making any progress.

He knew he should sit up and pull back the clutch lever, but instead, he felt himself being lifted up out of the tractor, into the dust and smoke above it. Then he was falling—tumbling down toward the earth. He felt his body smash against the hard ground.

———————

He was looking straight up into the sky—into the deep blue of twilight. He could feel the soothing coolness of the evening air on his face, but the warm smells of the day still lingered on. It was a sweet mixture.

He tried to lift his head but it wouldn't respond. At first he thought it might be one of those times when he woke up from a deep sleep, unable to move. Fighting through the panic, he would at last free one finger, then another, then an arm, until finally he had reclaimed his body. But this was different.

He watched the stars come out, and his thoughts drifted back to a clear summer night. He was a little boy, and his father had taken him outside to sleep under the stars. They lay side by side on the soft, damp grass, and watched as one star after another twinkled into existence.

He remembered trying to fix his gaze on one spot,

so that he could actually see a star becoming visible. But always they appeared in an area he had not been watching, and distracted him from his purpose.

He remembered how close they had been that night, how warm and safe he had felt lying next to his father. A thousand elves had danced around them in the dew-filled grass, while the sweet-smelling air perfumed their sleep, and the stars sent long quiet dreams down to soothe them. If only there had been more nights like that.

But now, as he lay under the fresh stars, something strange was happening in the clear, blackening sky above him.

The stars were disappearing.

What was more amazing, each one died the instant he looked at it—as if it were his direct stare that caused the star to lose its light.

He tried desperately to fix his gaze, the way he had tried on that night long ago, but it was no use. One by one, the bright stars caught his attention, and he looked at them, and they went out.